Pokémon Adventures™

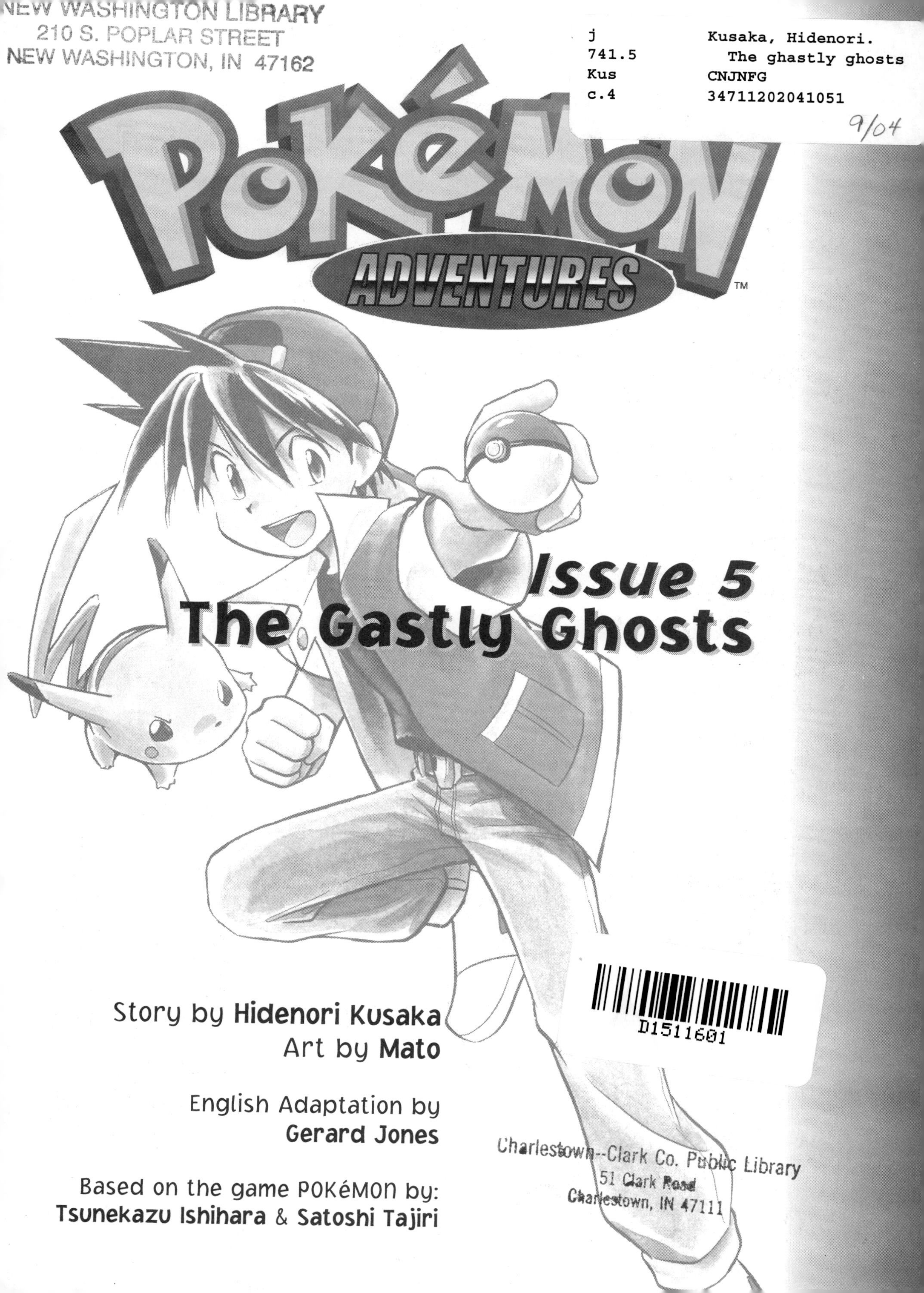

Issue 5
The Gastly Ghosts

Story by **Hidenori Kusaka**
Art by **Mato**

English Adaptation by
Gerard Jones

Based on the game POKéMON by:
Tsunekazu Ishihara & **Satoshi Tajiri**

POKéMON ADVENTURES
Issue 5:
The Gastly Ghosts

Story/Hidenori Kusaka
Art/Mato

English Adaptation/Gerard Jones

Translation/Kaori Inoue
Touch-up & Lettering/Dan Nakrosis
Graphics & Design/Carolina Ugalde
Editing/William Flanagan

Editor-in-Chief/Hyoe Narita
Publisher/Seiji Horibuchi

First published by
Shogakukan, Inc. in Japan.

© 1995, 1996 and 1998 Nintendo,
CREATURES, GAME FREAK.
™ & ® are trademarks of Nintendo.
© 2000 Nintendo.

The stories, characters, institutions
and incidents mentioned in this publication are entirely fictional. For the
purposes of publication in English,
the artwork in this publication is in
reverse from the original Japanese
version. Printed in Canada

Published by Viz Comics
P.O. Box 77010
San Francisco, CA 94107

For advertising opportunities, call:
Oliver Chin
Director of Sales and Marketing
(415) 546-7073 ext. 128

Ask for our free
Viz Shop-By-Mail catalog!
Call toll free: (800) 394-3042

CONTENTS

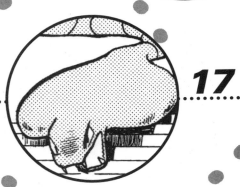

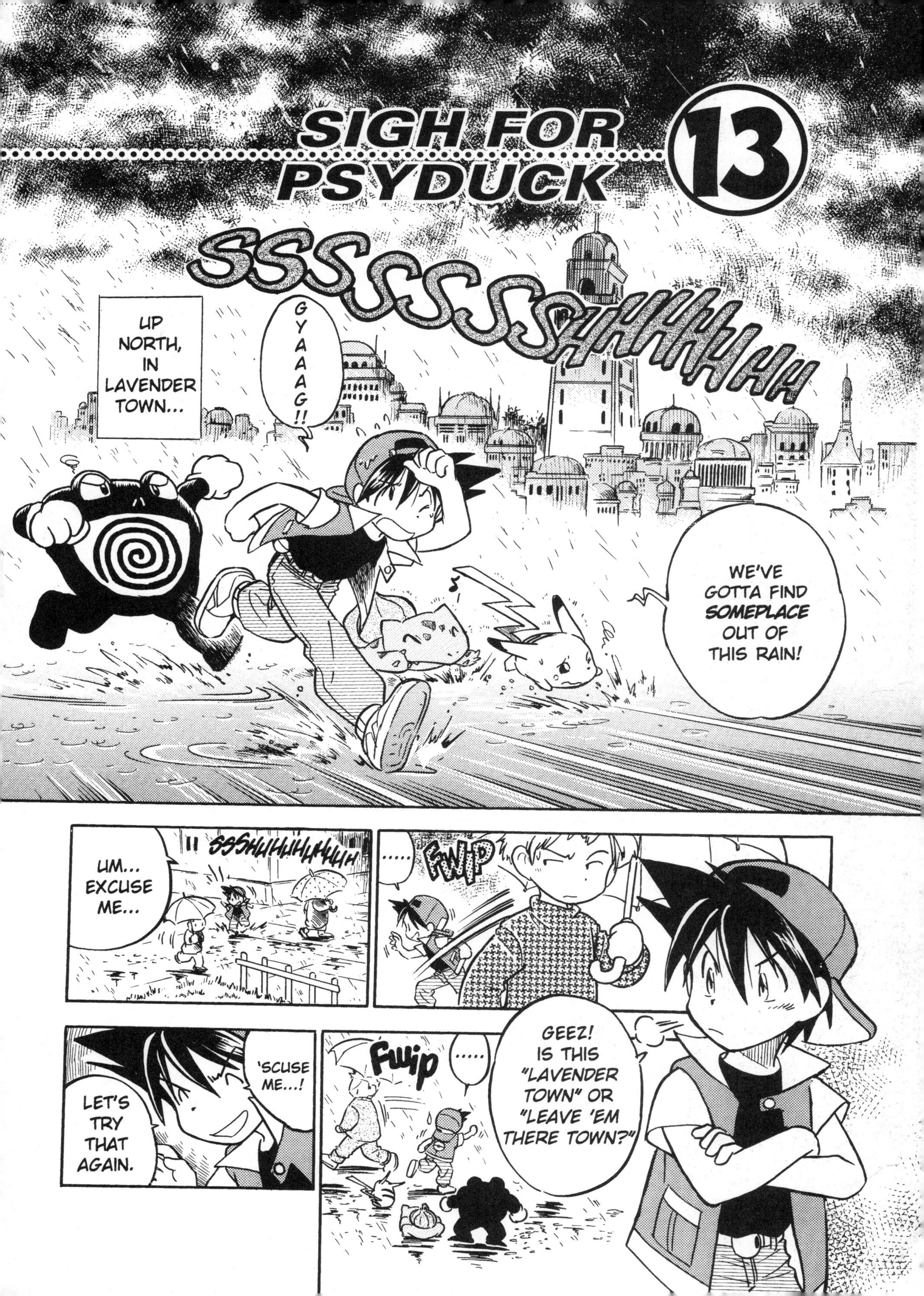
SIGH FOR PSYDUCK
13
SSSSSSSSHHHHHHHH
UP NORTH, IN LAVENDER TOWN...
GYAAAG!!
WE'VE GOTTA FIND SOMEPLACE OUT OF THIS RAIN!
SSSHHHHHHHHH
UM... EXCUSE ME...
.....
FWIP
'SCUSE ME...!
LET'S TRY THAT AGAIN.
Fwip
.....
GEEZ! IS THIS "LAVENDER TOWN" OR "LEAVE 'EM THERE TOWN?"

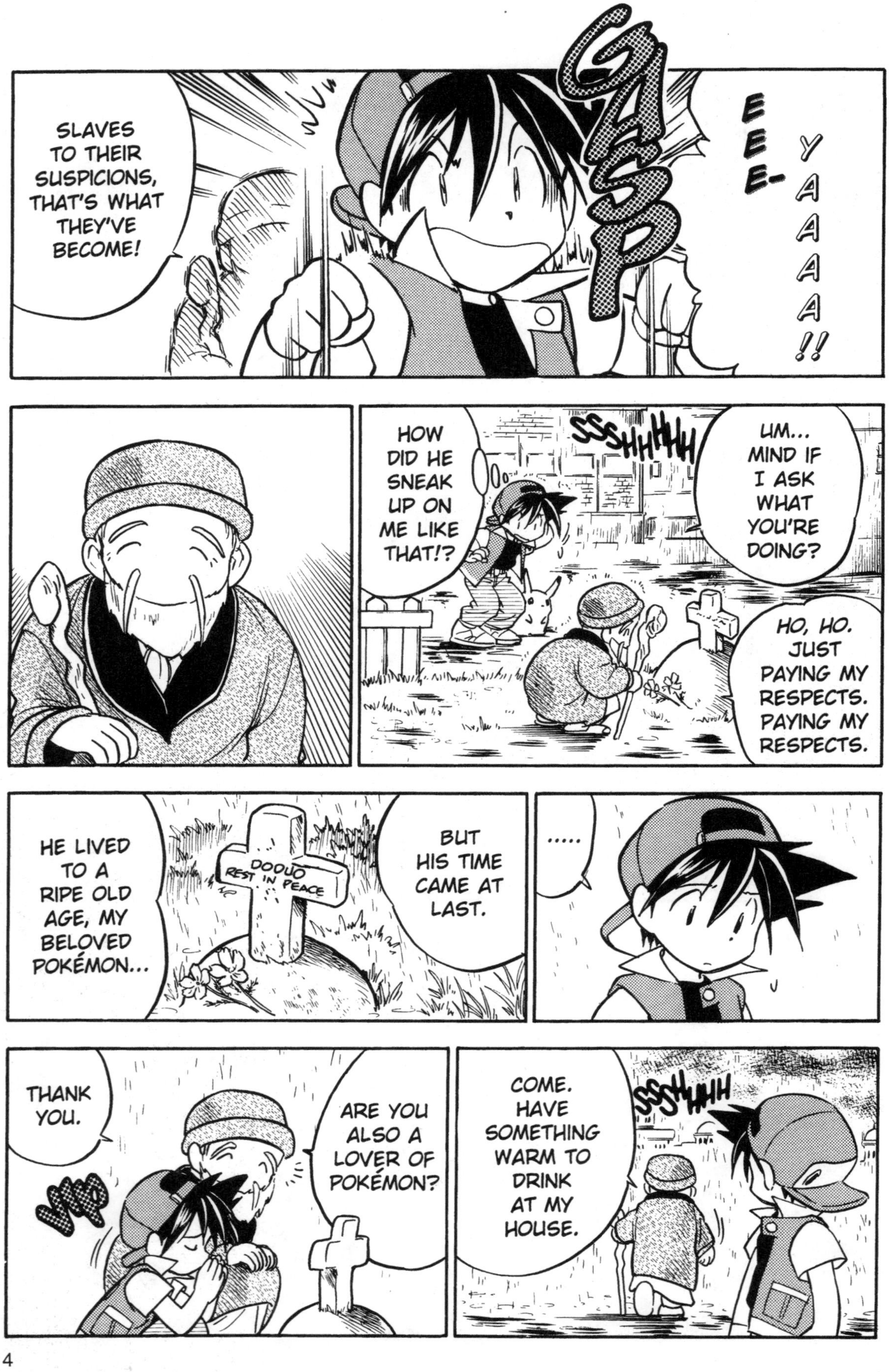
SLAVES TO THEIR SUSPICIONS, THAT'S WHAT THEY'VE BECOME!
GASP
EEE-YAAAAA!!
HOW DID HE SNEAK UP ON ME LIKE THAT!?
SSSHHHHH
UM... MIND IF I ASK WHAT YOU'RE DOING?
HO, HO. JUST PAYING MY RESPECTS. PAYING MY RESPECTS.
HE LIVED TO A RIPE OLD AGE, MY BELOVED POKÉMON...
DODUO REST IN PEACE
BUT HIS TIME CAME AT LAST.
.....
THANK YOU.
ARE YOU ALSO A LOVER OF POKÉMON?
SSSHHHH
COME. HAVE SOMETHING WARM TO DRINK AT MY HOUSE.

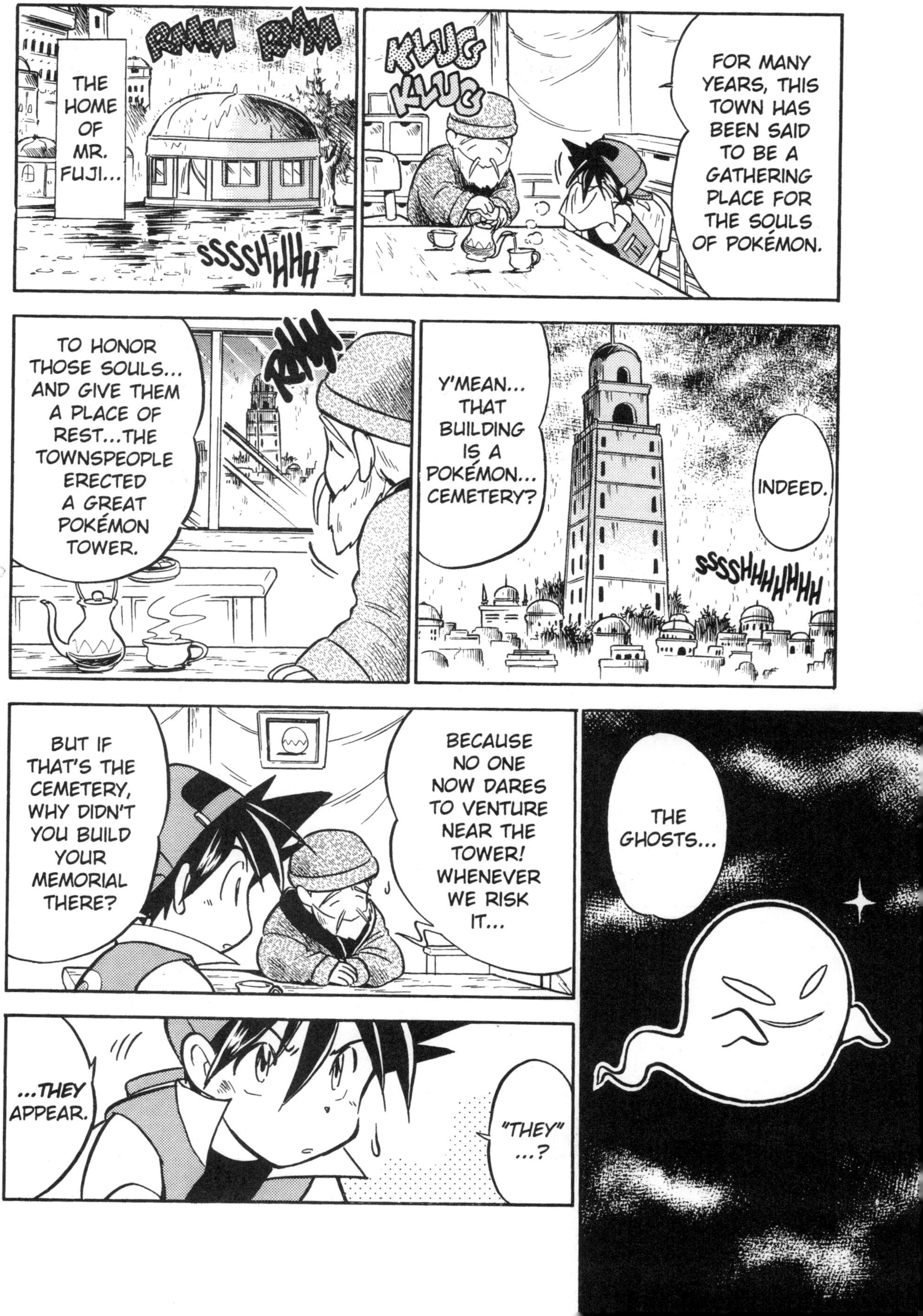
RAM RAM
THE HOME OF MR. FUJI...
SSSSHHHH
KLUG KLUG
FOR MANY YEARS, THIS TOWN HAS BEEN SAID TO BE A GATHERING PLACE FOR THE SOULS OF POKÉMON.
TO HONOR THOSE SOULS... AND GIVE THEM A PLACE OF REST...THE TOWNSPEOPLE ERECTED A GREAT POKÉMON TOWER.
RAM
Y'MEAN... THAT BUILDING IS A POKÉMON... CEMETERY?
INDEED.
SSSSHHHHHHHH
BUT IF THAT'S THE CEMETERY, WHY DIDN'T YOU BUILD YOUR MEMORIAL THERE?
BECAUSE NO ONE NOW DARES TO VENTURE NEAR THE TOWER! WHENEVER WE RISK IT...
...THEY APPEAR.
"THEY" ...?
THE GHOSTS...

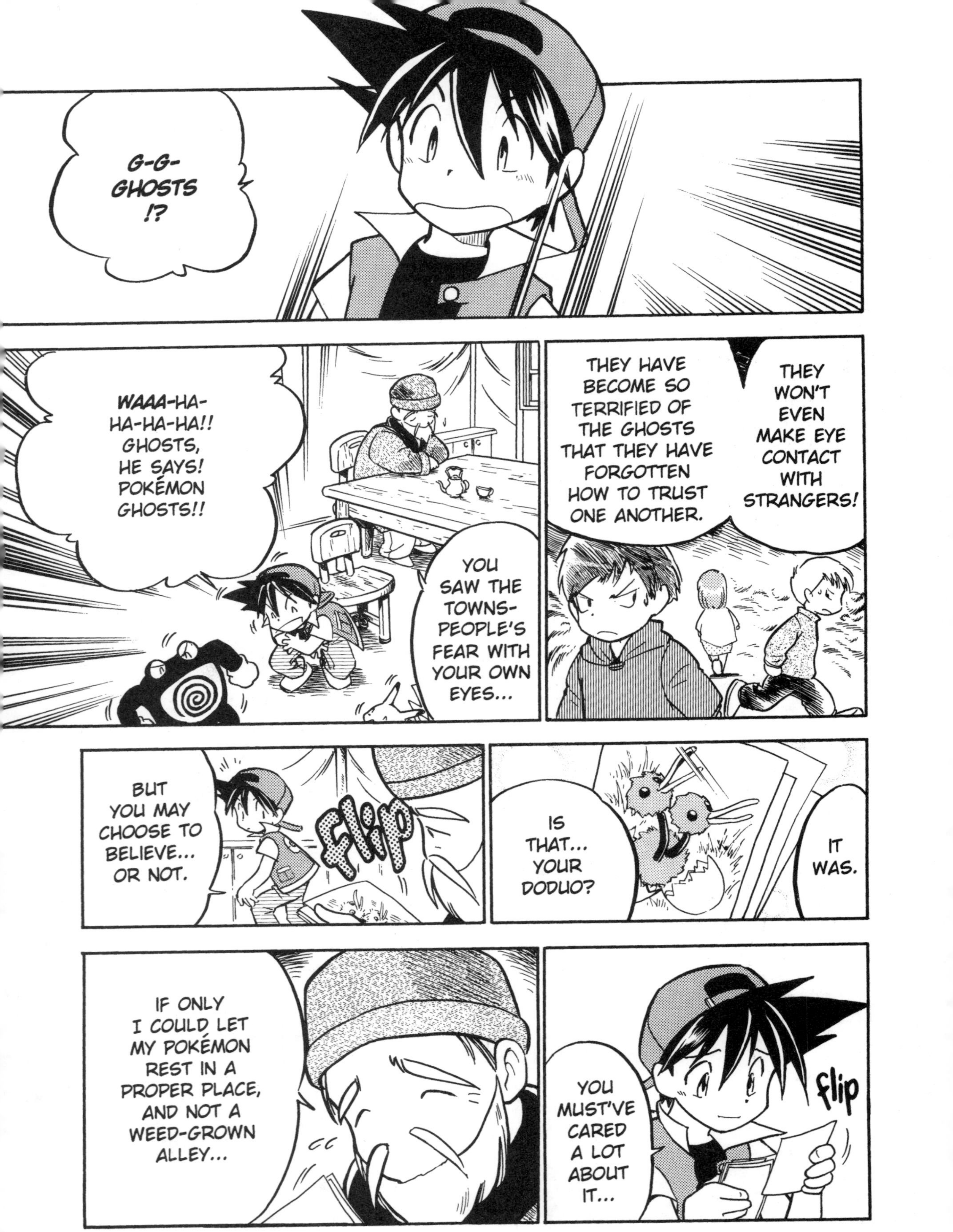
G-G-
GHOSTS
!?
WAAA-HA-
HA-HA-HA!!
GHOSTS,
HE SAYS!
POKÉMON
GHOSTS!!
YOU
SAW THE
TOWNS-
PEOPLE'S
FEAR WITH
YOUR OWN
EYES...
THEY HAVE
BECOME SO
TERRIFIED OF
THE GHOSTS
THAT THEY HAVE
FORGOTTEN
HOW TO TRUST
ONE ANOTHER.
THEY
WON'T
EVEN
MAKE EYE
CONTACT
WITH
STRANGERS!
BUT
YOU MAY
CHOOSE TO
BELIEVE...
OR NOT.
FLIP
IS
THAT...
YOUR
DODUO?
IT
WAS.
IF ONLY
I COULD LET
MY POKÉMON
REST IN A
PROPER PLACE,
AND NOT A
WEED-GROWN
ALLEY...
YOU
MUST'VE
CARED
A LOT
ABOUT
IT...
FLIP

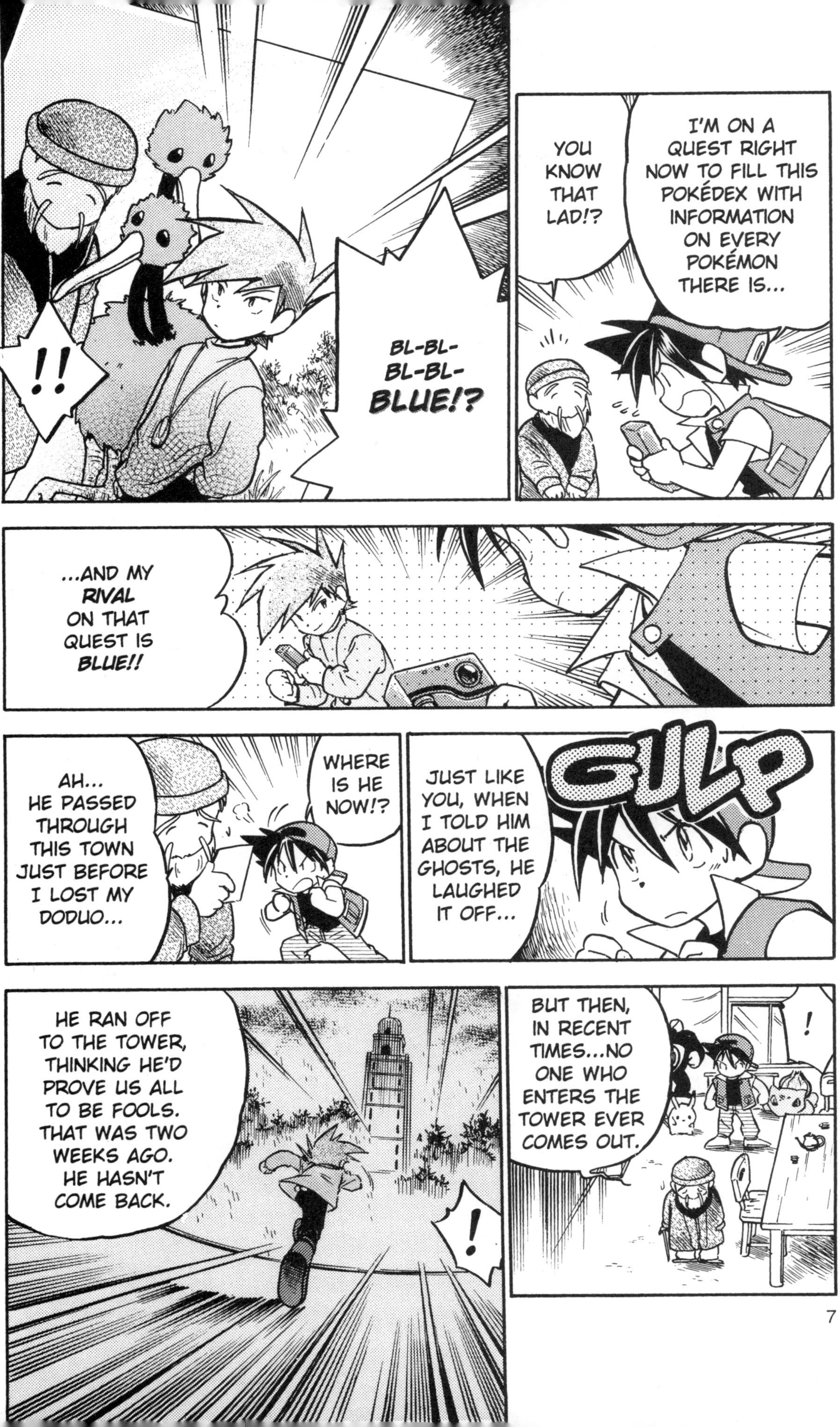
!!
BL-BL-BL-BL-BLUE!?
YOU KNOW THAT LAD!?
I'M ON A QUEST RIGHT NOW TO FILL THIS POKÉDEX WITH INFORMATION ON EVERY POKÉMON THERE IS...
...AND MY RIVAL ON THAT QUEST IS BLUE!!
AH... HE PASSED THROUGH THIS TOWN JUST BEFORE I LOST MY DODUO...
WHERE IS HE NOW!?
JUST LIKE YOU, WHEN I TOLD HIM ABOUT THE GHOSTS, HE LAUGHED IT OFF...
GULP
HE RAN OFF TO THE TOWER, THINKING HE'D PROVE US ALL TO BE FOOLS. THAT WAS TWO WEEKS AGO. HE HASN'T COME BACK.
!
BUT THEN, IN RECENT TIMES...NO ONE WHO ENTERS THE TOWER EVER COMES OUT.
!

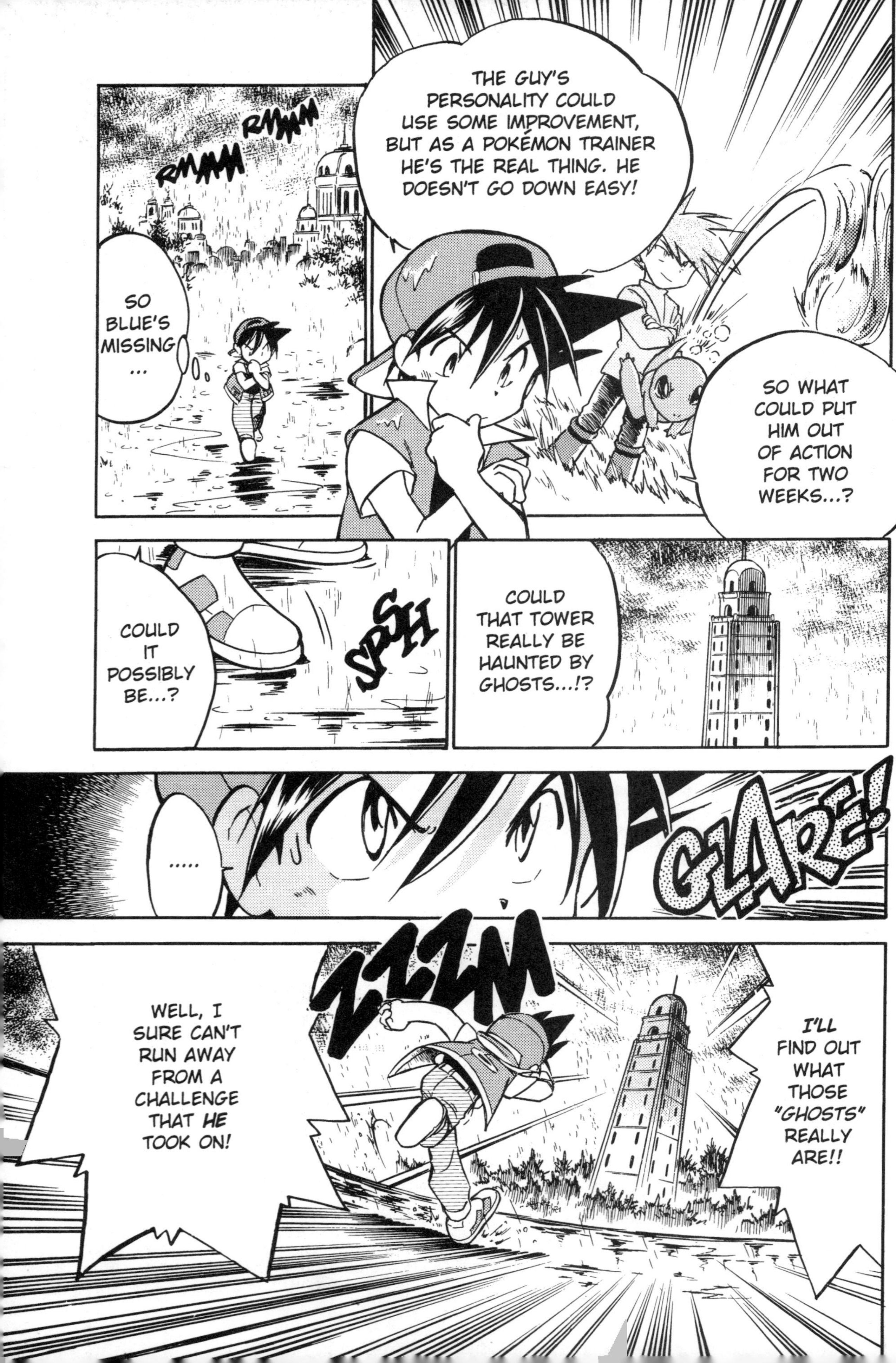
RMMM
RMMM
SO BLUE'S MISSING ...
THE GUY'S PERSONALITY COULD USE SOME IMPROVEMENT, BUT AS A POKÉMON TRAINER HE'S THE REAL THING. HE DOESN'T GO DOWN EASY!
SO WHAT COULD PUT HIM OUT OF ACTION FOR TWO WEEKS...?
COULD IT POSSIBLY BE...?
SPSH
COULD THAT TOWER REALLY BE HAUNTED BY GHOSTS...!?
.....
GLARE!
ZZZM
WELL, I SURE CAN'T RUN AWAY FROM A CHALLENGE THAT *HE* TOOK ON!
I'LL FIND OUT WHAT THOSE *"GHOSTS"* REALLY ARE!!

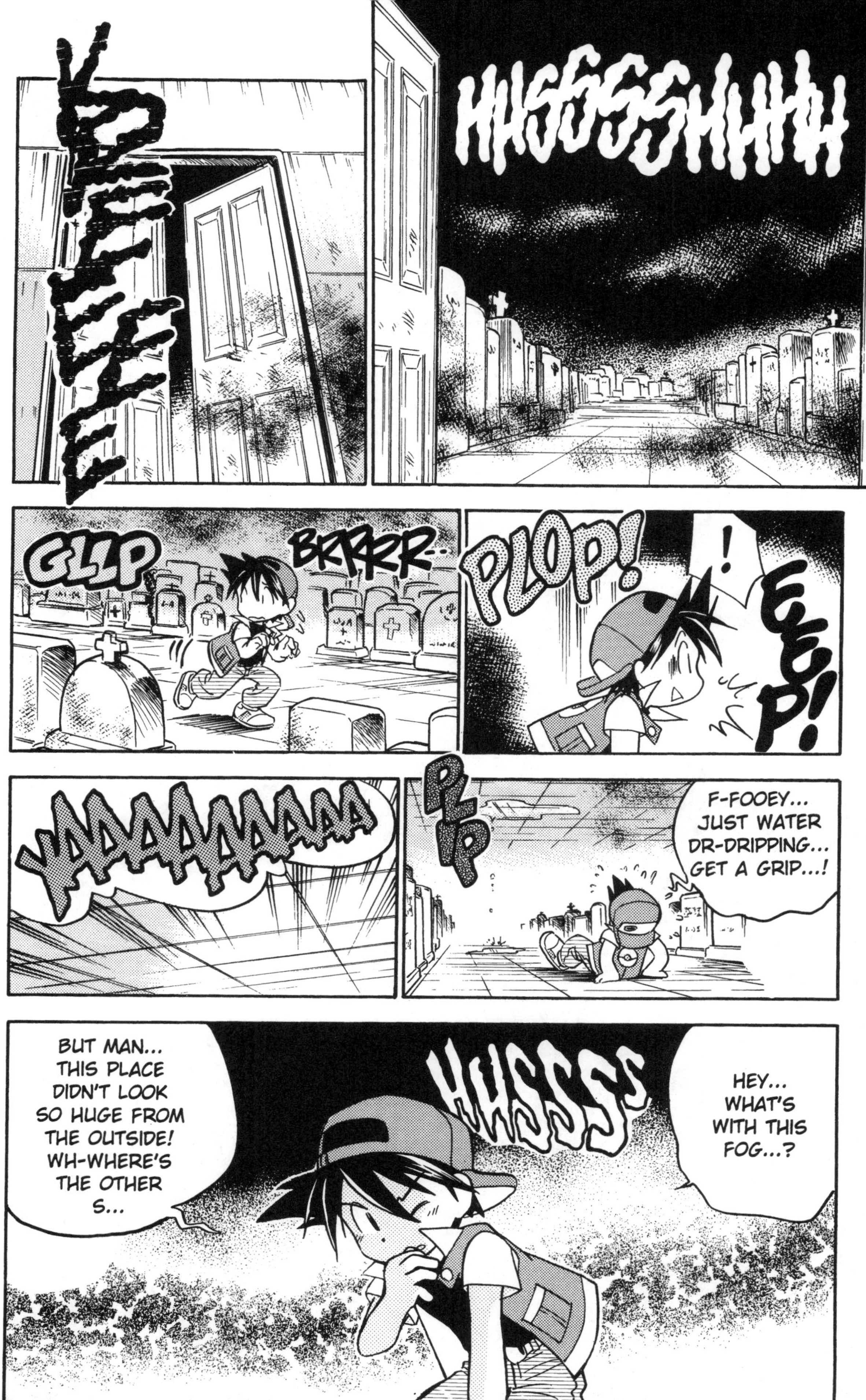
GLIP
BRRRR..
PLOP!
!
PLIP
F-FOOEY... JUST WATER DR-DRIPPING... GET A GRIP...!
BUT MAN... THIS PLACE DIDN'T LOOK SO HUGE FROM THE OUTSIDE! WH-WHERE'S THE OTHER S...
HWSSSS
HEY... WHAT'S WITH THIS FOG...?

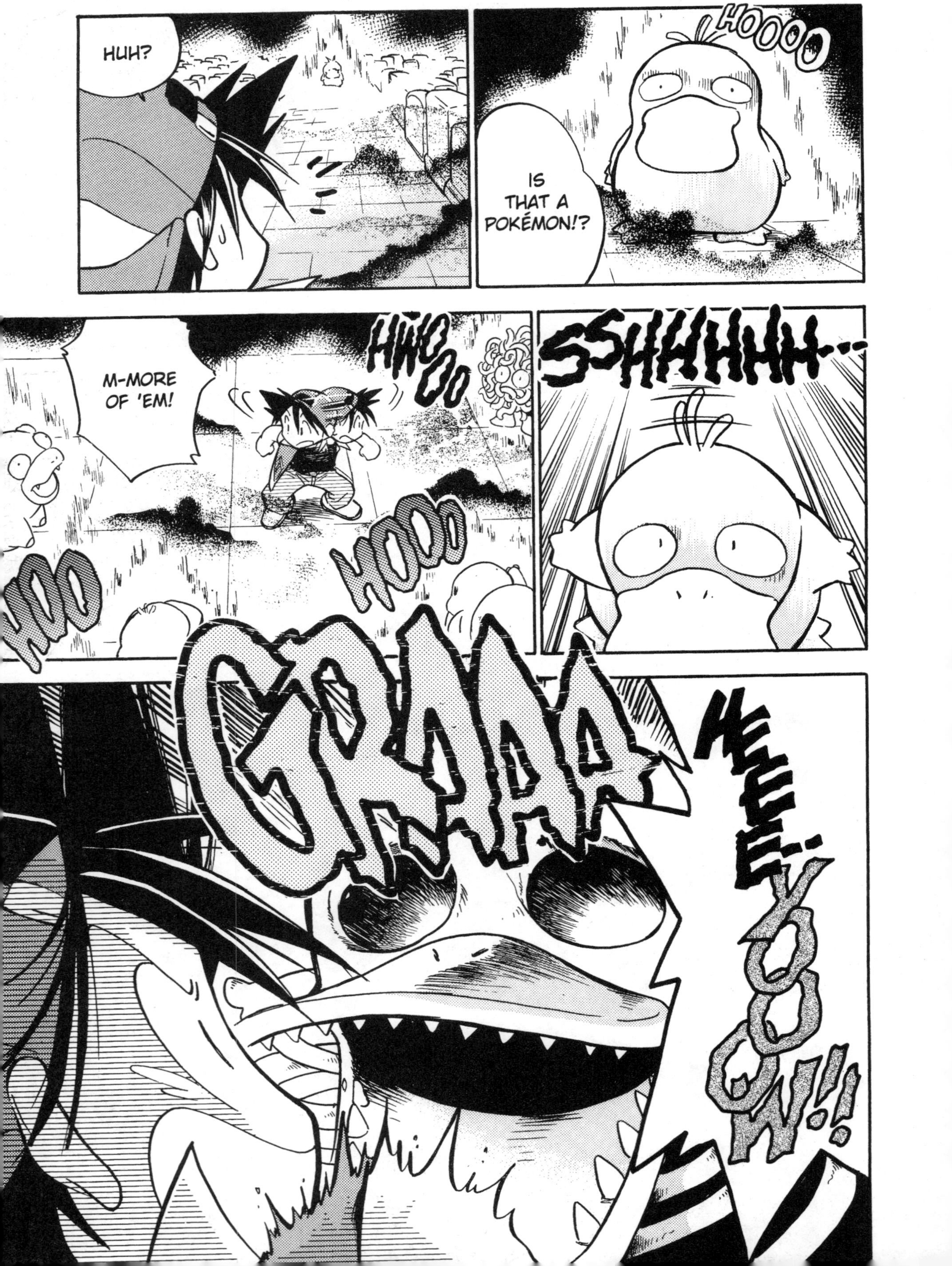
HUH?
HOOOO
IS THAT A POKÉMON!?
M-MORE OF 'EM!
HWOOO
SSHHHHH...
HOO
HOOO
GRAAA
HEEEEYOOOW!!

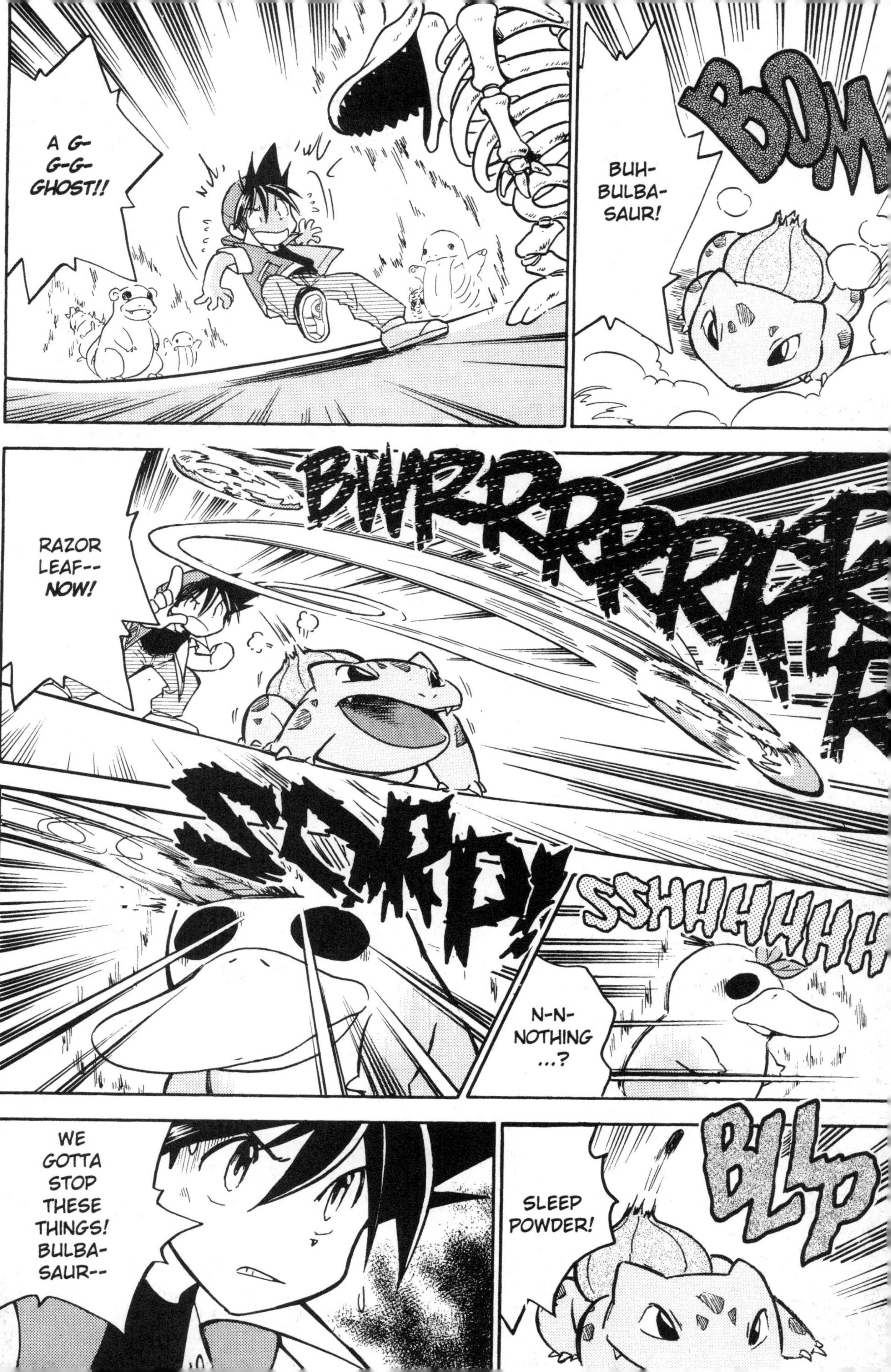

A G-
G-G-
GHOST!!
BOOM
BUH-
BULBA-
SAUR!
BWRRRRRRR
RAZOR
LEAF--
NOW!
SCRPP!
SSHHHHHH
N-N-
NOTHING
...?
WE
GOTTA
STOP
THESE
THINGS!
BULBA-
SAUR--
BLP
SLEEP
POWDER!

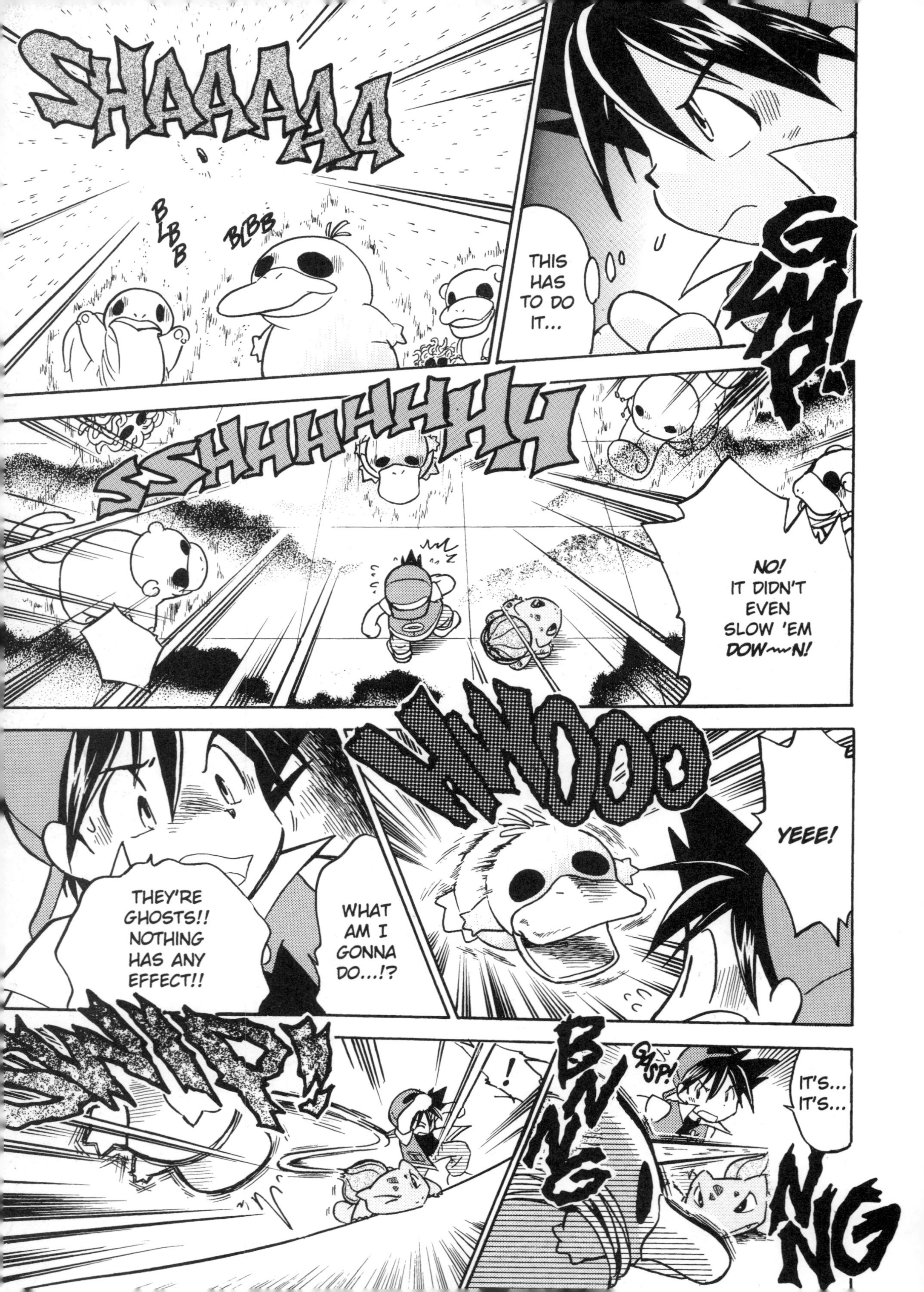
SHAAAAA
BLBB
BLBB
THIS HAS TO DO IT...
GMP!
SSHHHHHHH
NO! IT DIDN'T EVEN SLOW 'EM DOW~~N!
WHOOO
YEEE!
THEY'RE GHOSTS!! NOTHING HAS ANY EFFECT!!
WHAT AM I GONNA DO...!?
SHIP!
!
GASP!
BWNG
IT'S... IT'S...
NG

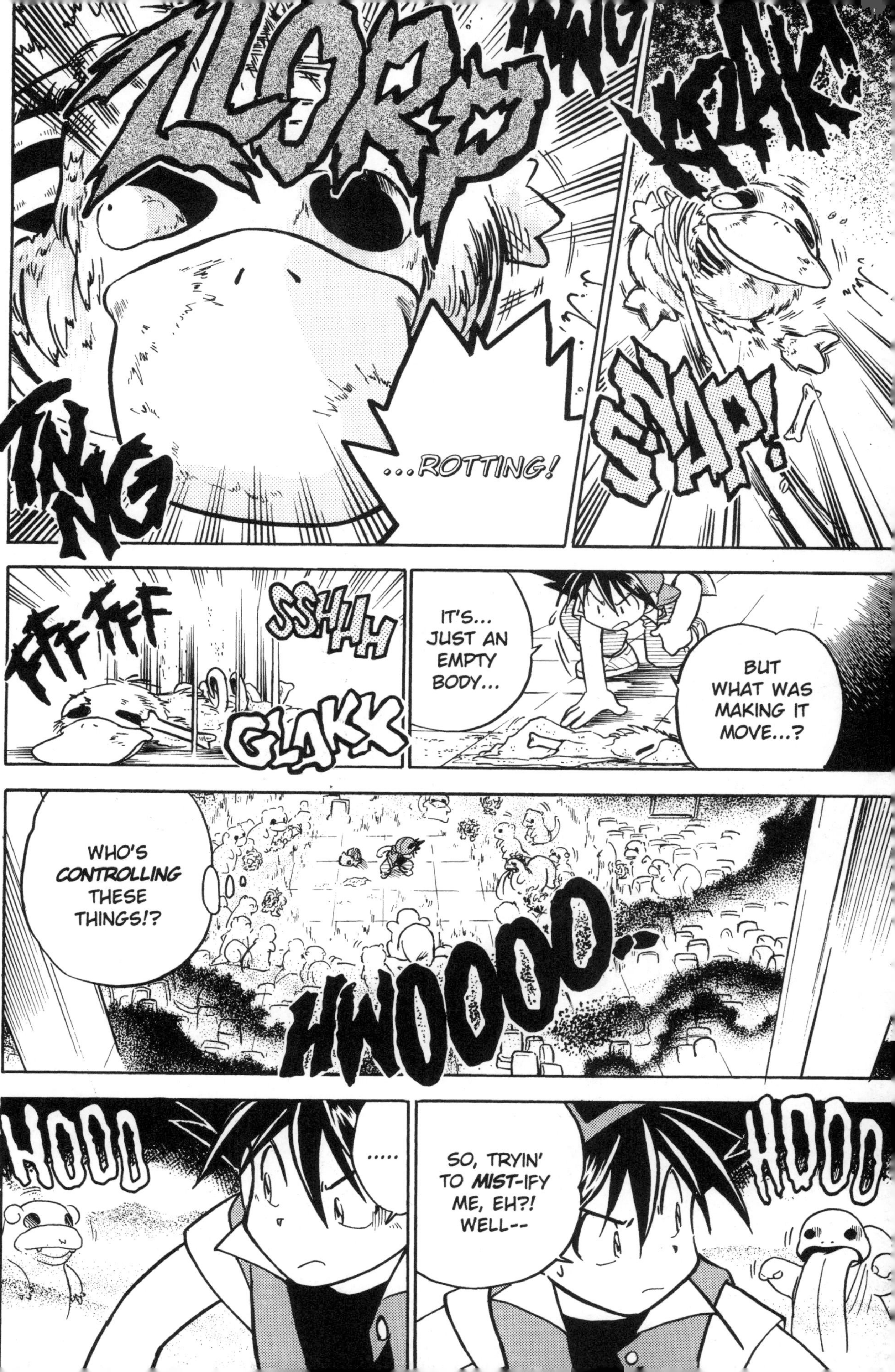
ZLORP
...ROTTING!
SNAP!
FFF FFF
SSHHH
GLAKK
IT'S... JUST AN EMPTY BODY...
BUT WHAT WAS MAKING IT MOVE...?
WHO'S CONTROLLING THESE THINGS!?
HWOOOO
HOOO
.....
SO, TRYIN' TO MIST-IFY ME, EH?! WELL--
HOOO

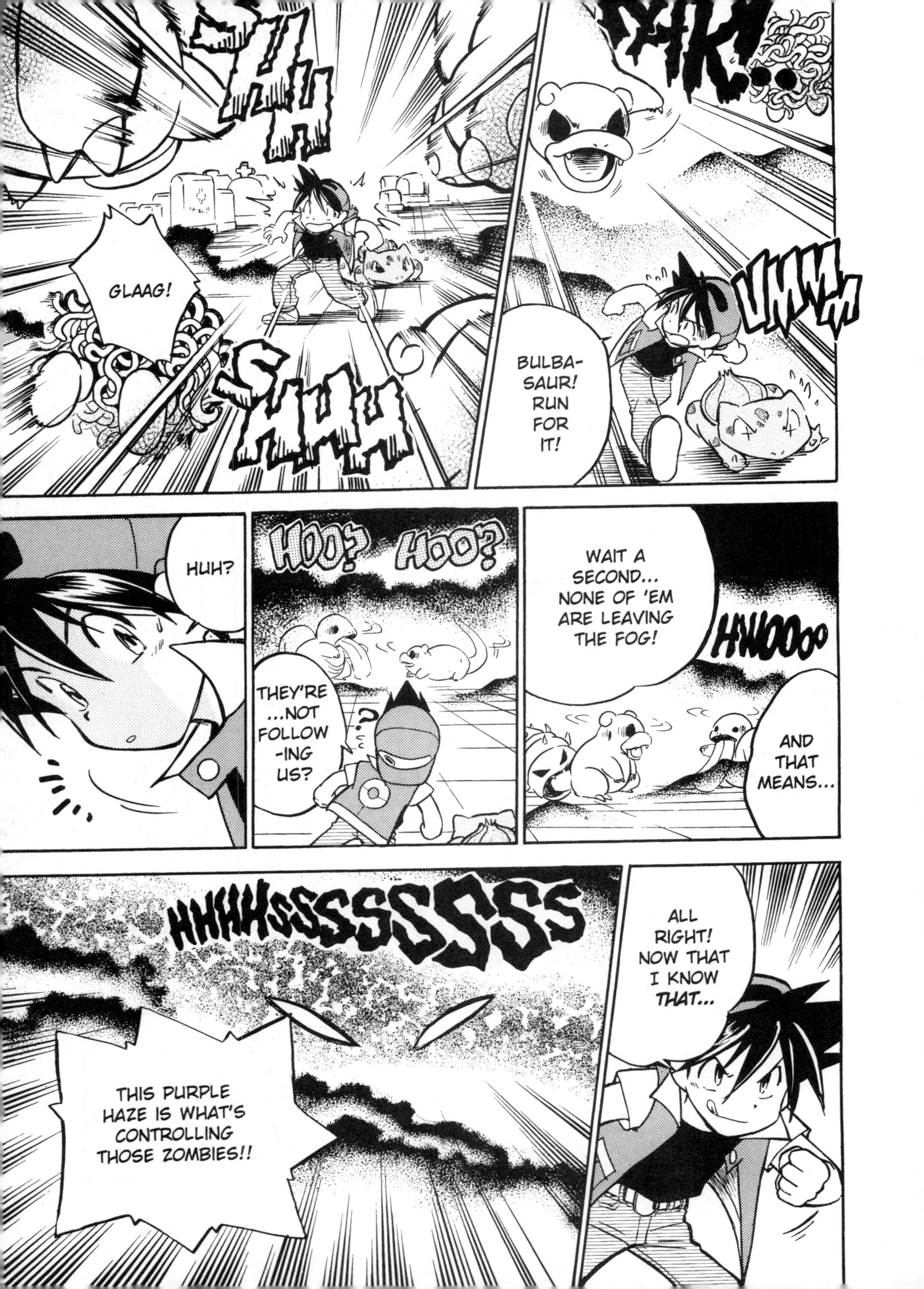

ZHHH
GLAAG!
SHHH
THK!
UMMM
BULBA-SAUR! RUN FOR IT!
HUH?
HOO? HOO?
THEY'RE ...NOT FOLLOW-ING US?
WAIT A SECOND... NONE OF 'EM ARE LEAVING THE FOG!
HWOOOO
AND THAT MEANS...
HHHHSSSSSSSS
ALL RIGHT! NOW THAT I KNOW THAT...
THIS PURPLE HAZE IS WHAT'S CONTROLLING THOSE ZOMBIES!!

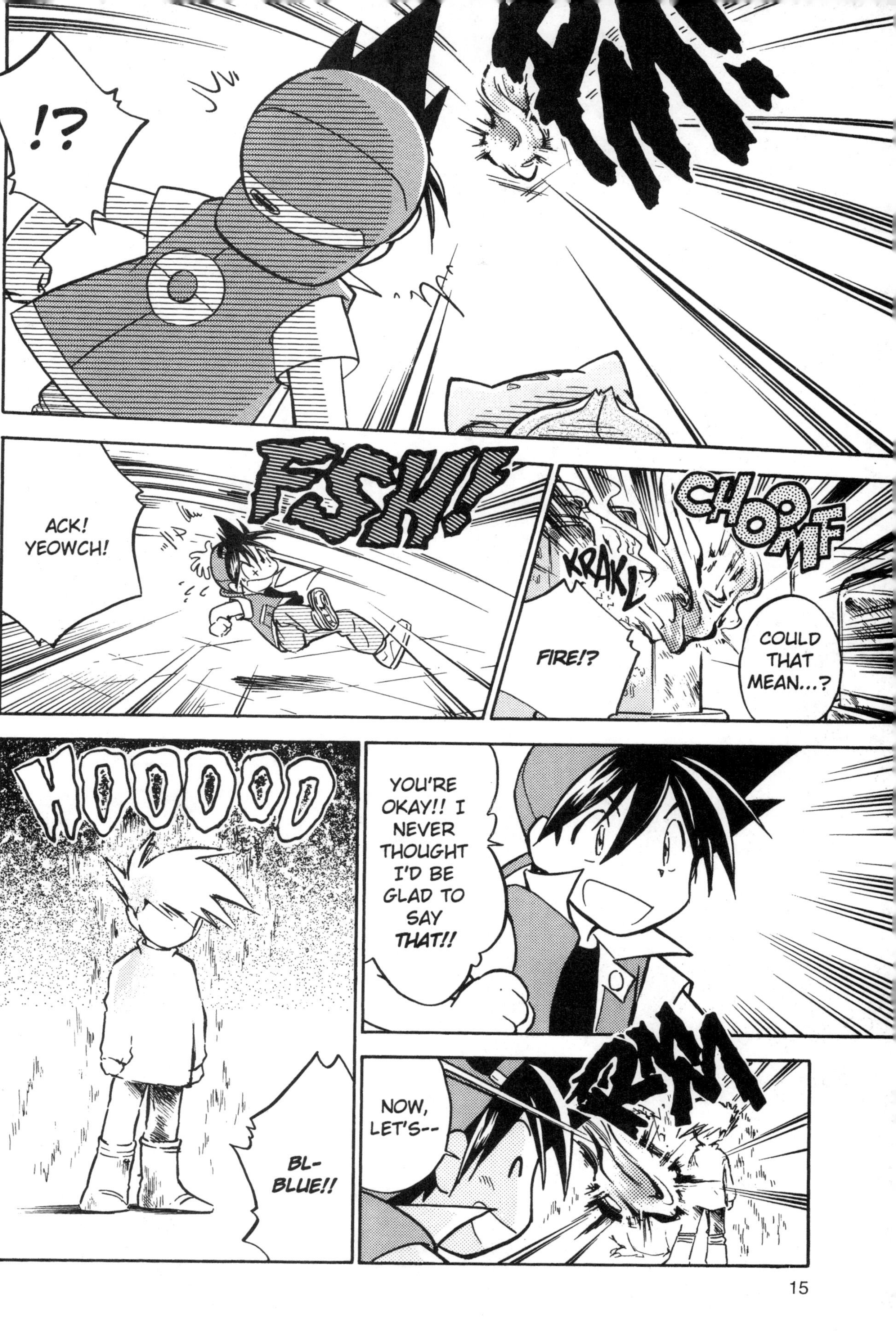
!?
ACK! YEOWCH!
CHOOMF
KRAKL
FIRE!?
COULD THAT MEAN...?
YOU'RE OKAY!! I NEVER THOUGHT I'D BE GLAD TO SAY THAT!!
BL- BLUE!!
NOW, LET'S--

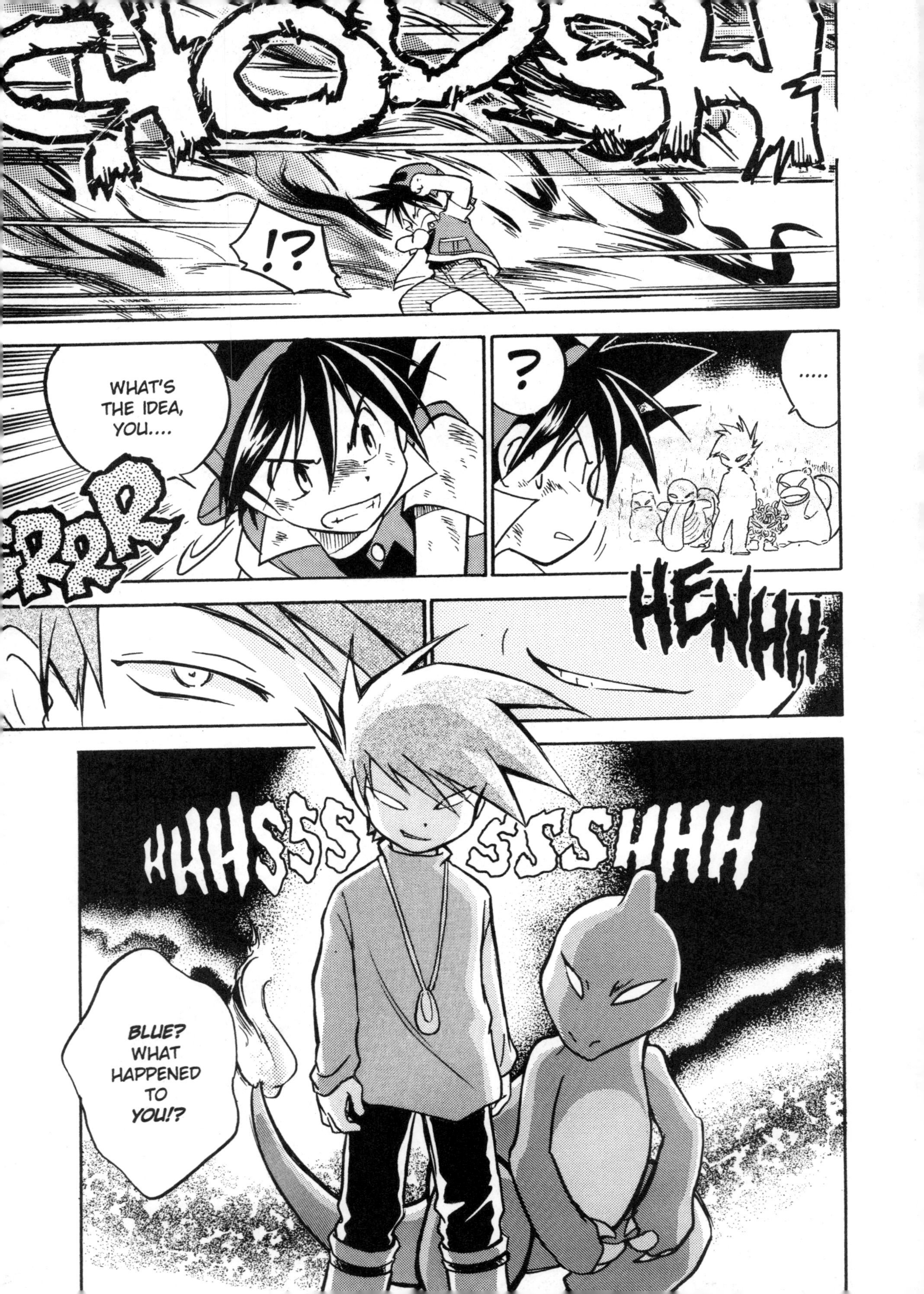
WHOOSH
!?
WHAT'S THE IDEA, YOU....
GRRR
?
.....
HENHH
HHHSSSSSSSHHH
BLUE? WHAT HAPPENED TO YOU!?

THAT AWFUL ARBOK! 14

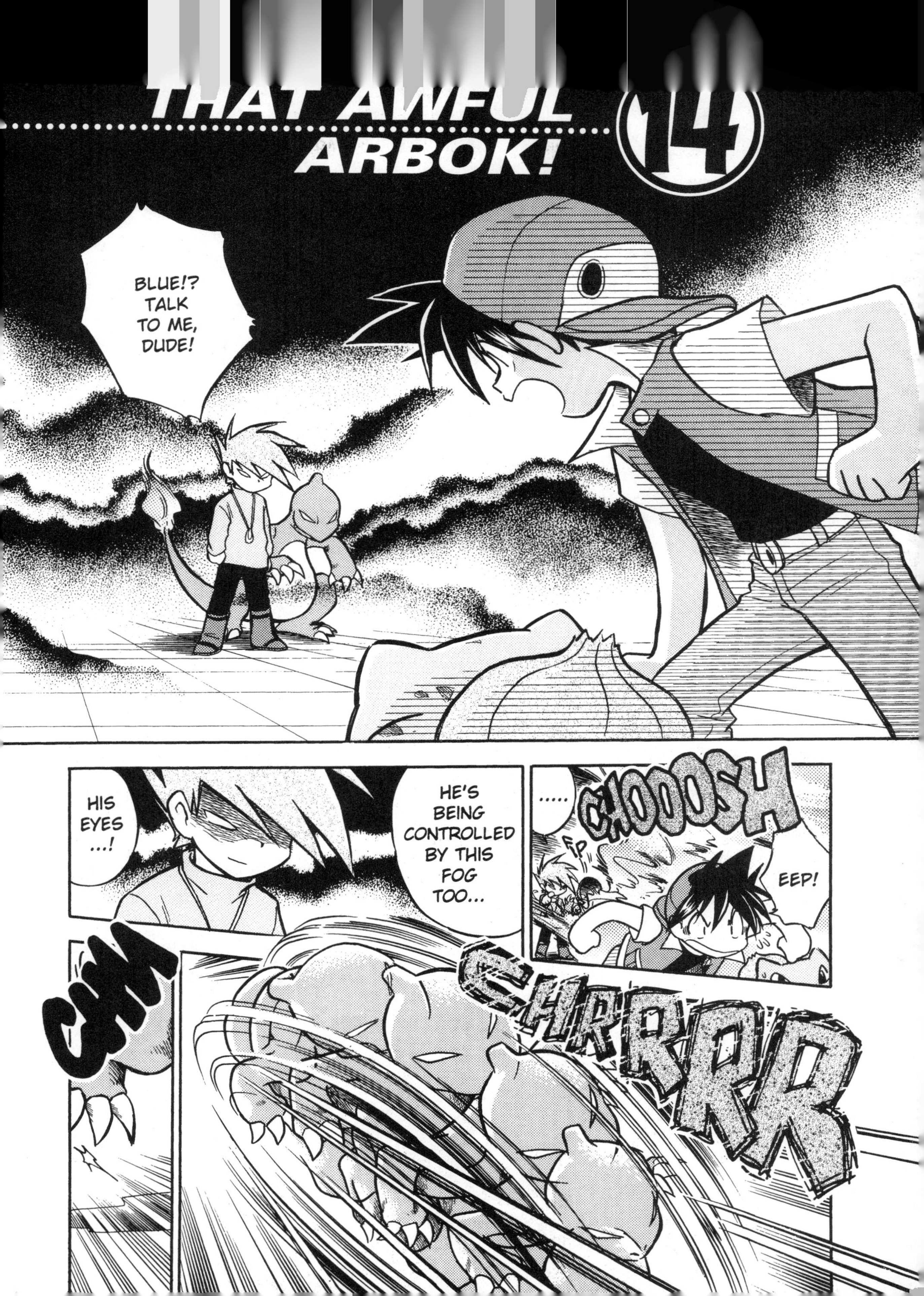
BLUE!? TALK TO ME, DUDE!
HIS EYES ...!
HE'S BEING CONTROLLED BY THIS FOG TOO...
.....
CHOOOSH
FIP
EEP!
SHRRRR

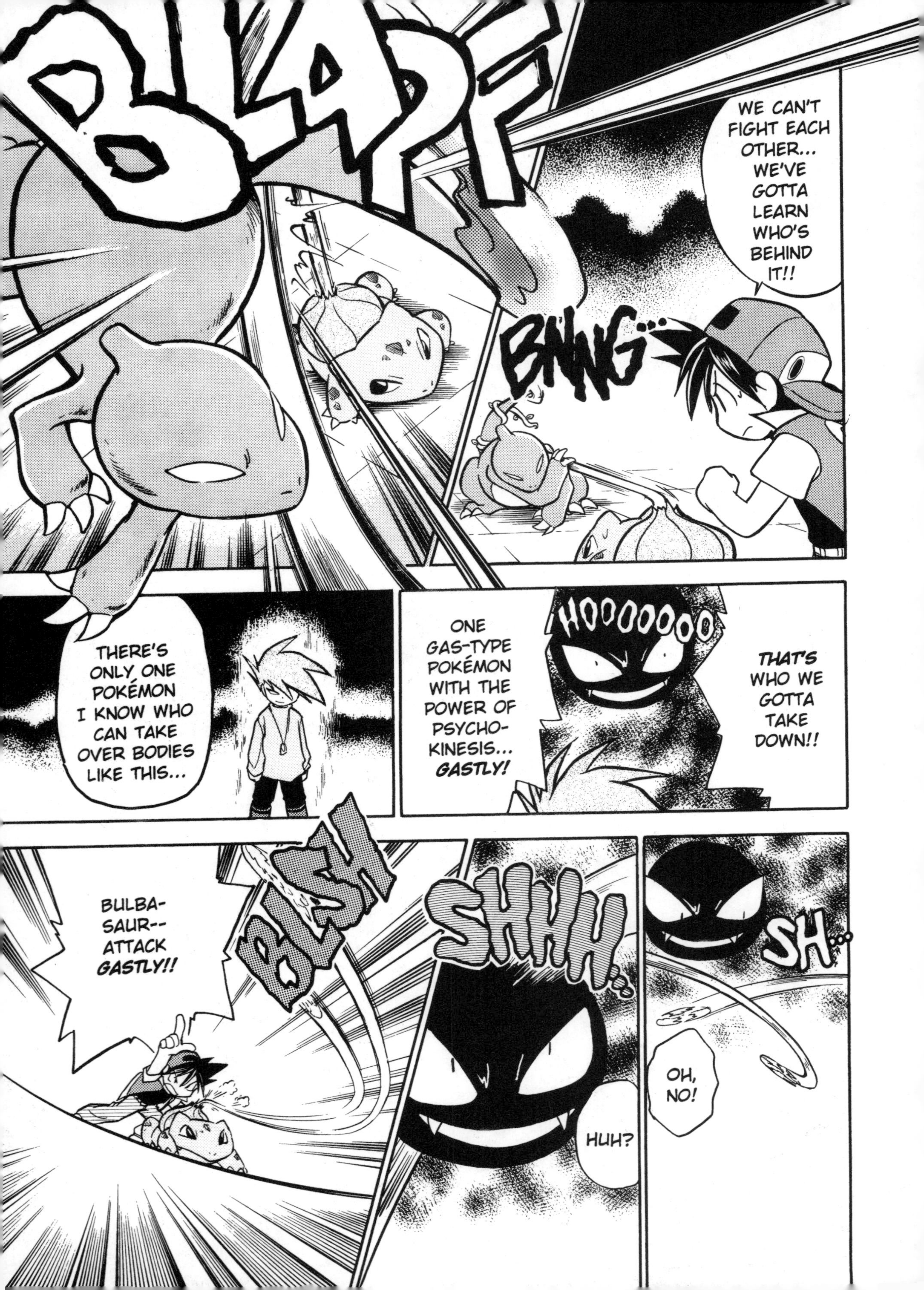
BLAPP
WE CAN'T FIGHT EACH OTHER... WE'VE GOTTA LEARN WHO'S BEHIND IT!!
BANG...
THERE'S ONLY ONE POKÉMON I KNOW WHO CAN TAKE OVER BODIES LIKE THIS...
ONE GAS-TYPE POKÉMON WITH THE POWER OF PSYCHO-KINESIS... GASTLY!
HOOOOOOO
THAT'S WHO WE GOTTA TAKE DOWN!!
BULBA-SAUR--ATTACK GASTLY!!
BLISH
SHHH...
SH...
OH, NO!
HUH?

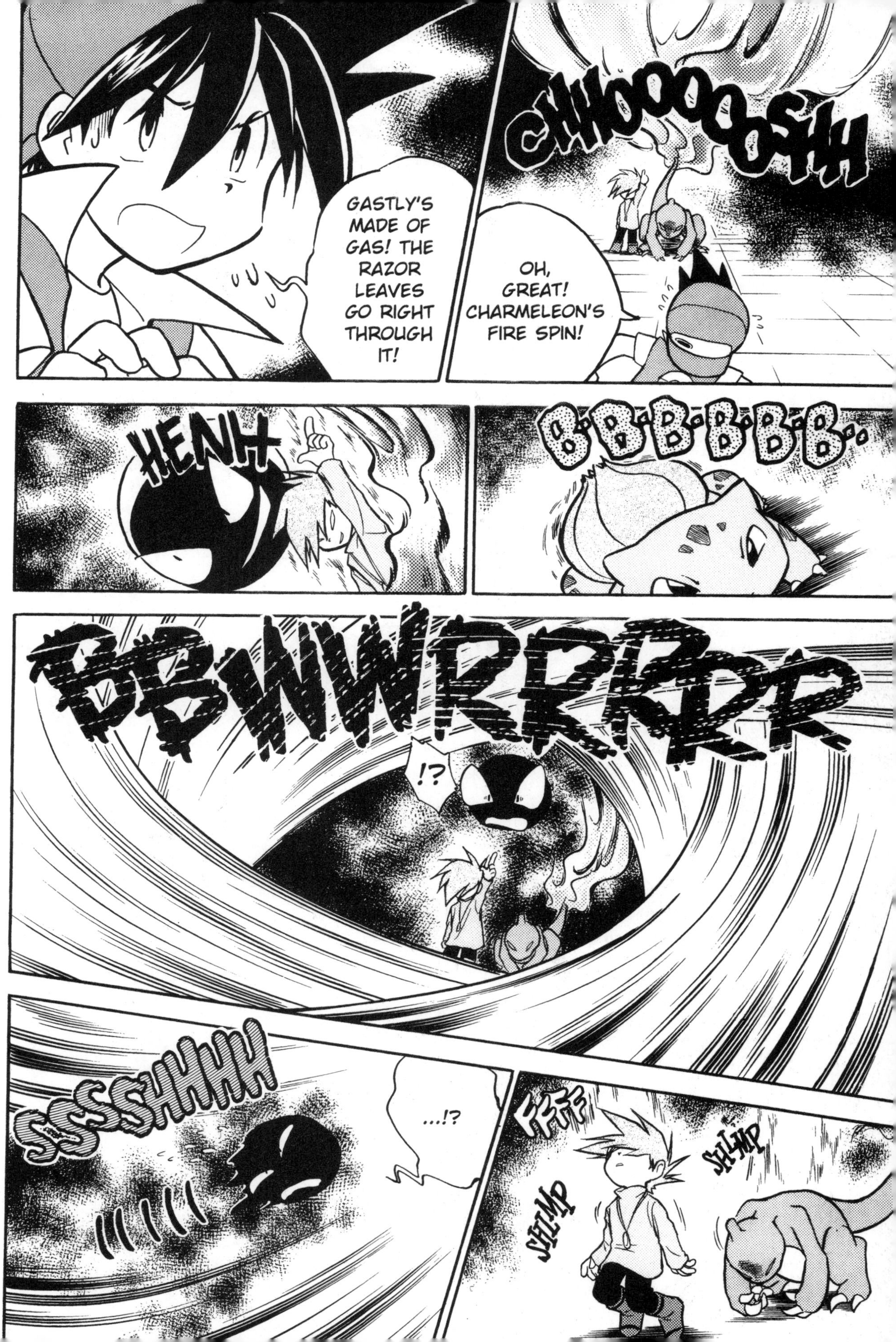
CHHOOOOOSHH
GASTLY'S MADE OF GAS! THE RAZOR LEAVES GO RIGHT THROUGH IT!
OH, GREAT! CHARMELEON'S FIRE SPIN!
BBBBBBB...
HENH
BBWWRRRRR
!?
...!?
SSSSHHHH
FFF
SHLMP
SHLMP

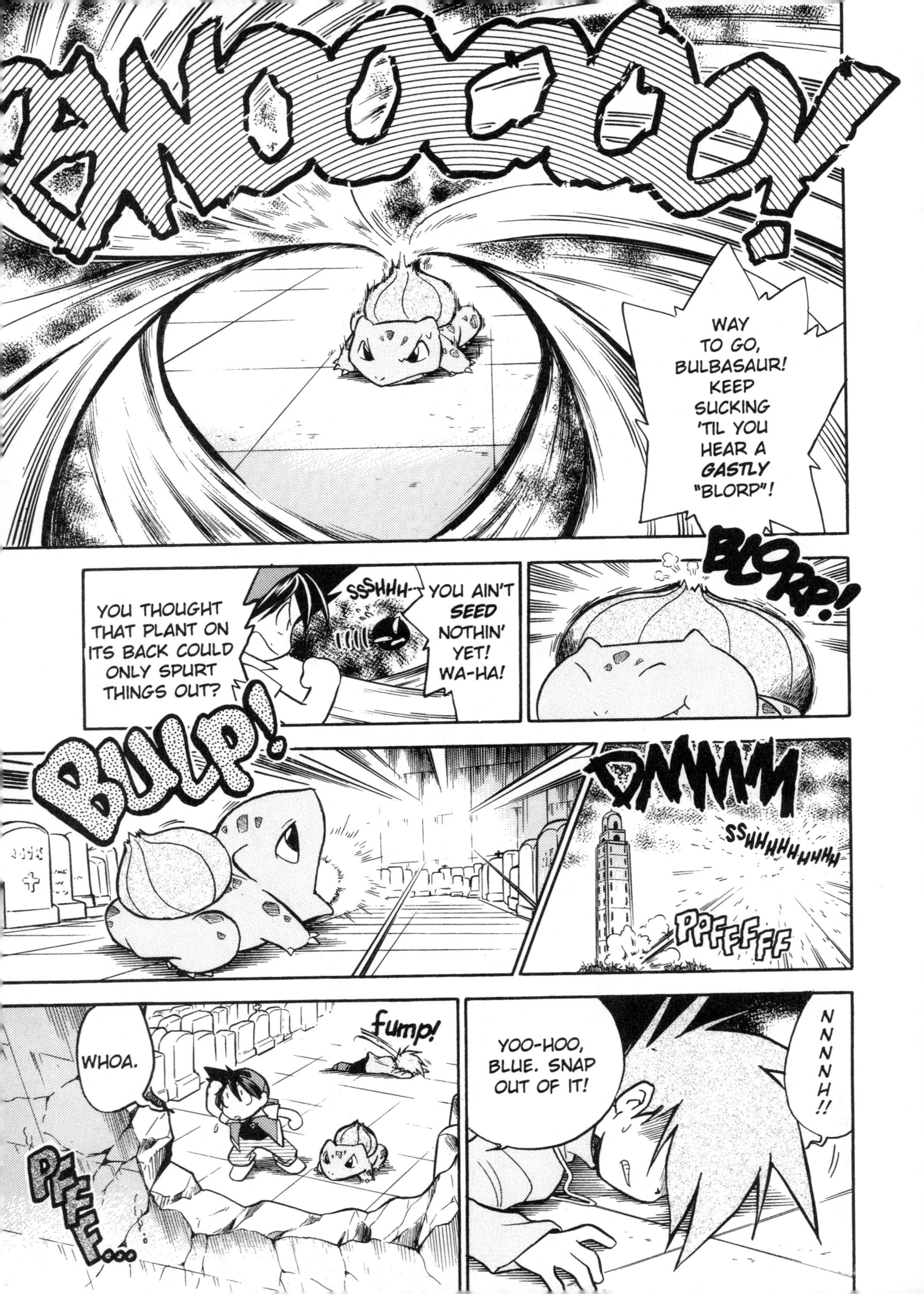
BWOOOOOOX!
WAY TO GO, BULBASAUR! KEEP SUCKING 'TIL YOU HEAR A GASTLY "BLORP"!
YOU THOUGHT THAT PLANT ON ITS BACK COULD ONLY SPURT THINGS OUT?
SSSHHH
YOU AIN'T SEED NOTHIN' YET! WA-HA!
BLORRP!
BULP!
DMMMM
SSHHHHHHHHH
PPFFFFFF
WHOA.
fump!
PFFFT...
YOO-HOO, BLUE. SNAP OUT OF IT!
NNNNH!!

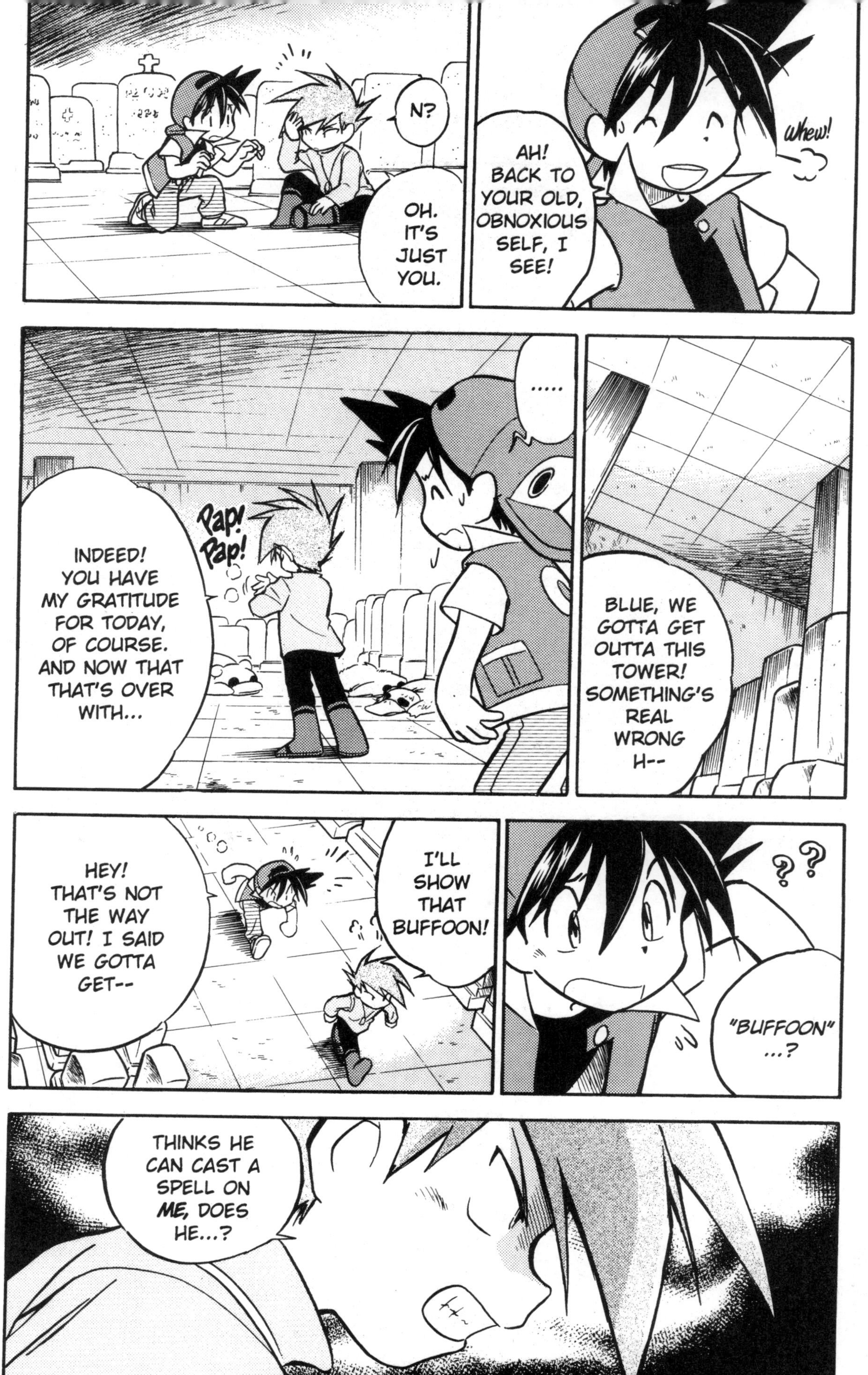
N?
OH. IT'S JUST YOU.
AH! BACK TO YOUR OLD, OBNOXIOUS SELF, I SEE!
Whew!
.....
INDEED! YOU HAVE MY GRATITUDE FOR TODAY, OF COURSE. AND NOW THAT THAT'S OVER WITH...
Pap! Pap!
BLUE, WE GOTTA GET OUTTA THIS TOWER! SOMETHING'S REAL WRONG H--
I'LL SHOW THAT BUFFOON!
HEY! THAT'S NOT THE WAY OUT! I SAID WE GOTTA GET--
"BUFFOON" ...?
THINKS HE CAN CAST A SPELL ON *ME*, DOES HE...?

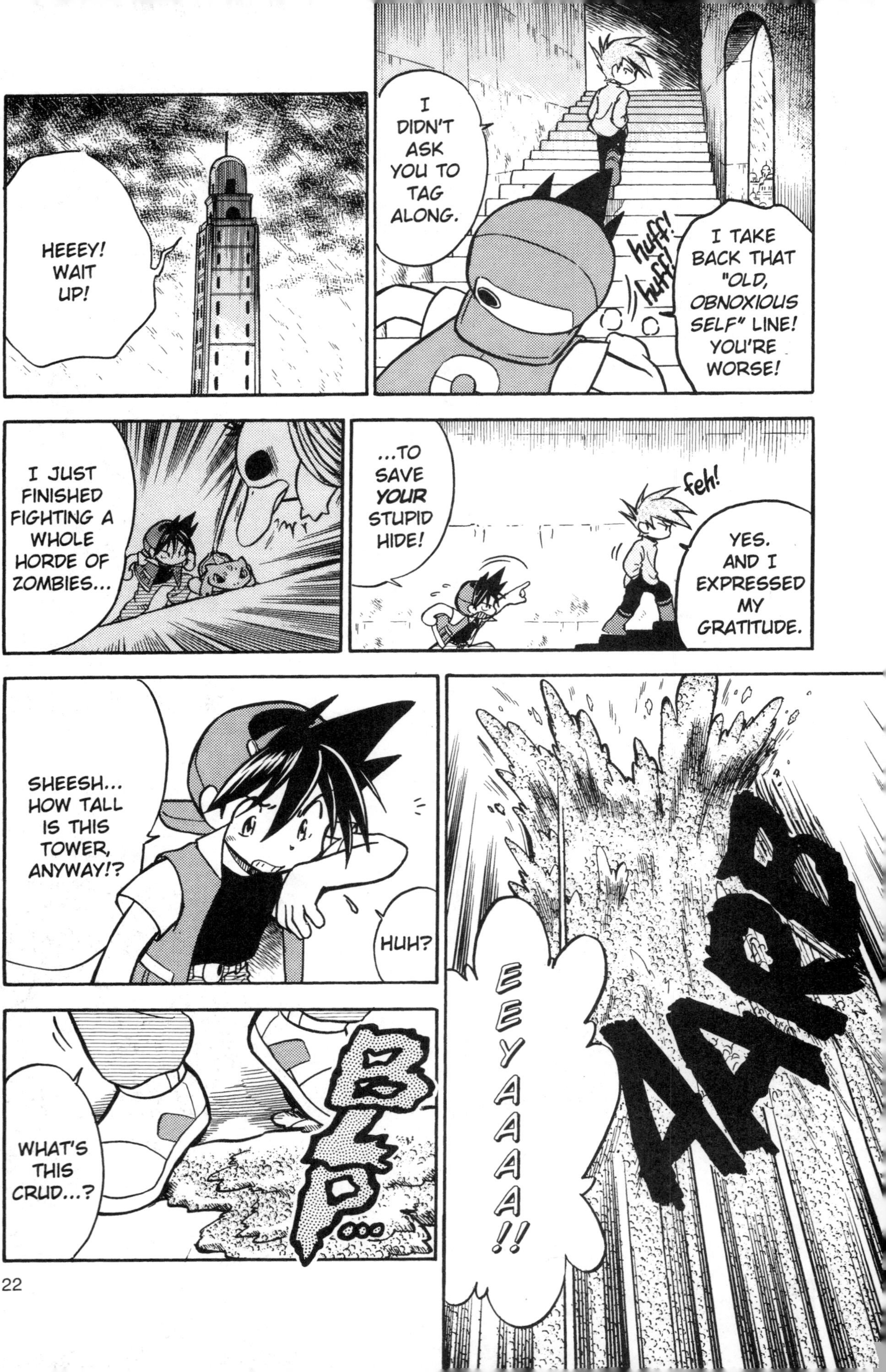
HEEEY! WAIT UP!
I DIDN'T ASK YOU TO TAG ALONG.
huff! huff!
I TAKE BACK THAT "OLD, OBNOXIOUS SELF" LINE! YOU'RE WORSE!
I JUST FINISHED FIGHTING A WHOLE HORDE OF ZOMBIES...
...TO SAVE YOUR STUPID HIDE!
feh!
YES. AND I EXPRESSED MY GRATITUDE.
SHEESH... HOW TALL IS THIS TOWER, ANYWAY!?
HUH?
WHAT'S THIS CRUD...?
BLOP...
EEYAAAAA!!

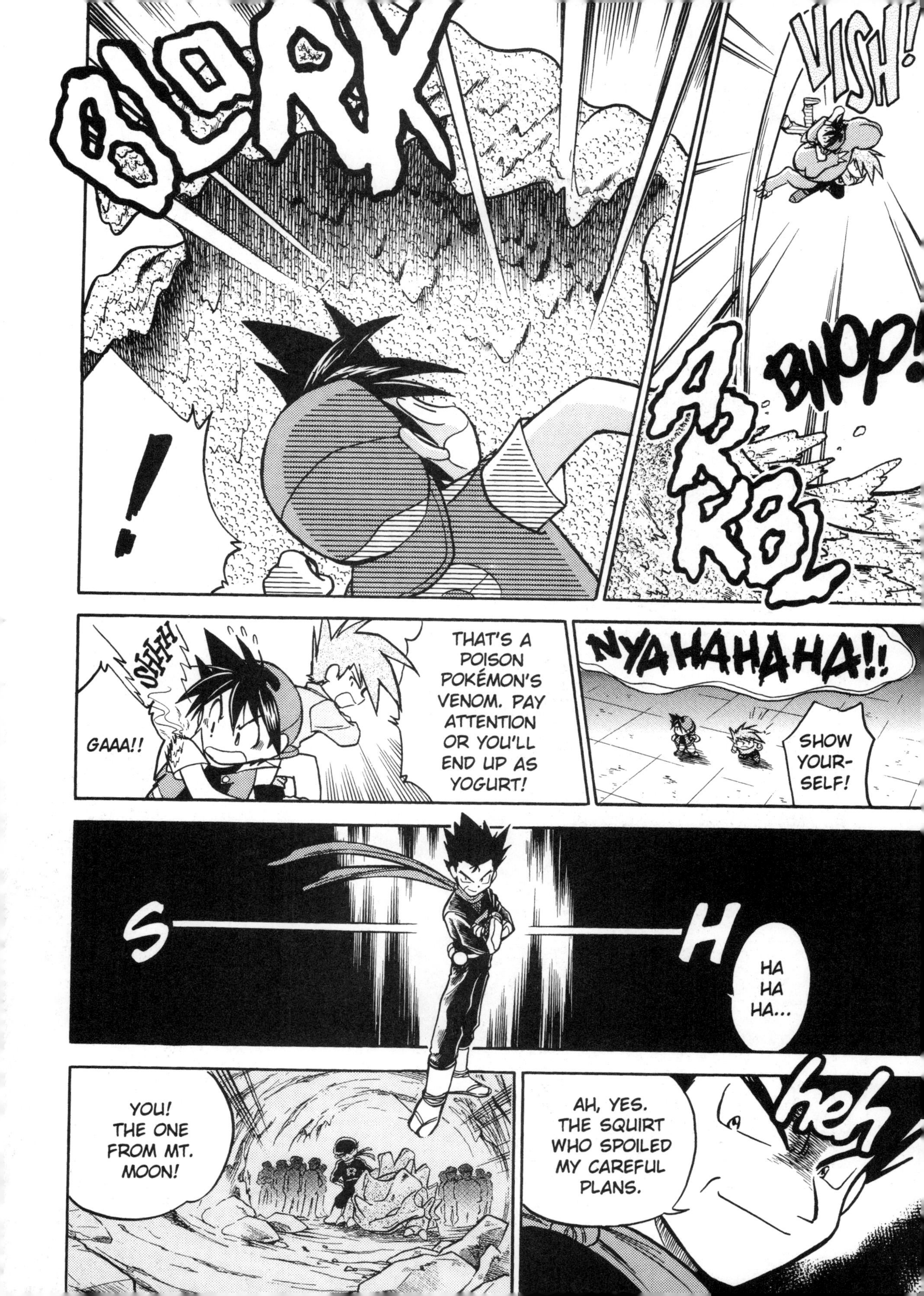
VISH!
BWOP!
!
SHHH
GAAA!!
THAT'S A POISON POKÉMON'S VENOM. PAY ATTENTION OR YOU'LL END UP AS YOGURT!
NYAHAHAHA!!
SHOW YOURSELF!
S
H
HA HA HA...
YOU! THE ONE FROM MT. MOON!
AH, YES. THE SQUIRT WHO SPOILED MY CAREFUL PLANS.
heh

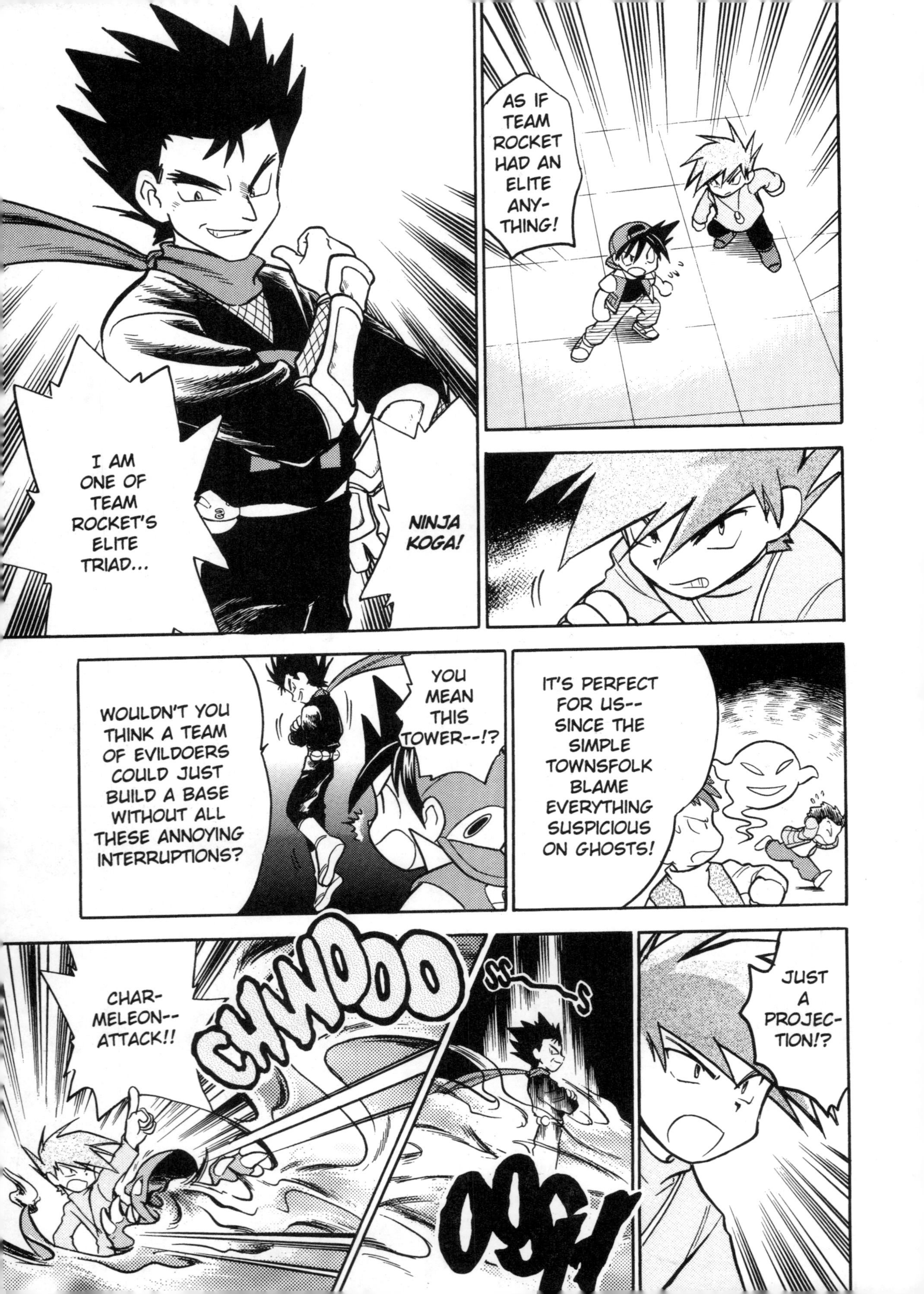
I AM ONE OF TEAM ROCKET'S ELITE TRIAD...
NINJA KOGA!
AS IF TEAM ROCKET HAD AN ELITE ANY-THING!
WOULDN'T YOU THINK A TEAM OF EVILDOERS COULD JUST BUILD A BASE WITHOUT ALL THESE ANNOYING INTERRUPTIONS?
YOU MEAN THIS TOWER--!?
IT'S PERFECT FOR US--SINCE THE SIMPLE TOWNSFOLK BLAME EVERYTHING SUSPICIOUS ON GHOSTS!
CHAR-MELEON--ATTACK!!
CHWOOO
JUST A PROJEC-TION!?

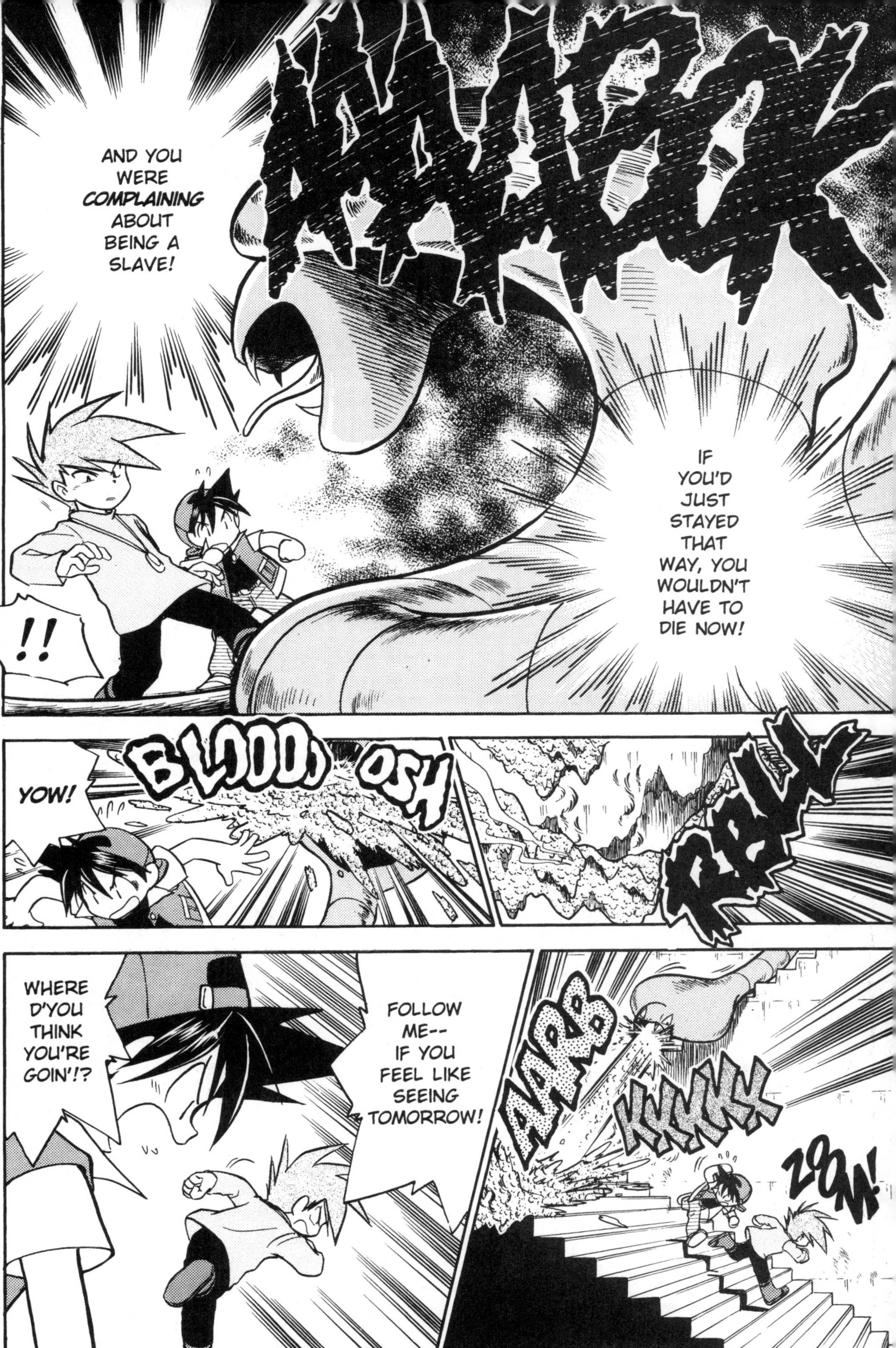
AND YOU WERE COMPLAINING ABOUT BEING A SLAVE!
IF YOU'D JUST STAYED THAT WAY, YOU WOULDN'T HAVE TO DIE NOW!
!!
YOW!
WHERE D'YOU THINK YOU'RE GOIN'!?
FOLLOW ME-- IF YOU FEEL LIKE SEEING TOMORROW!
ZOOM!

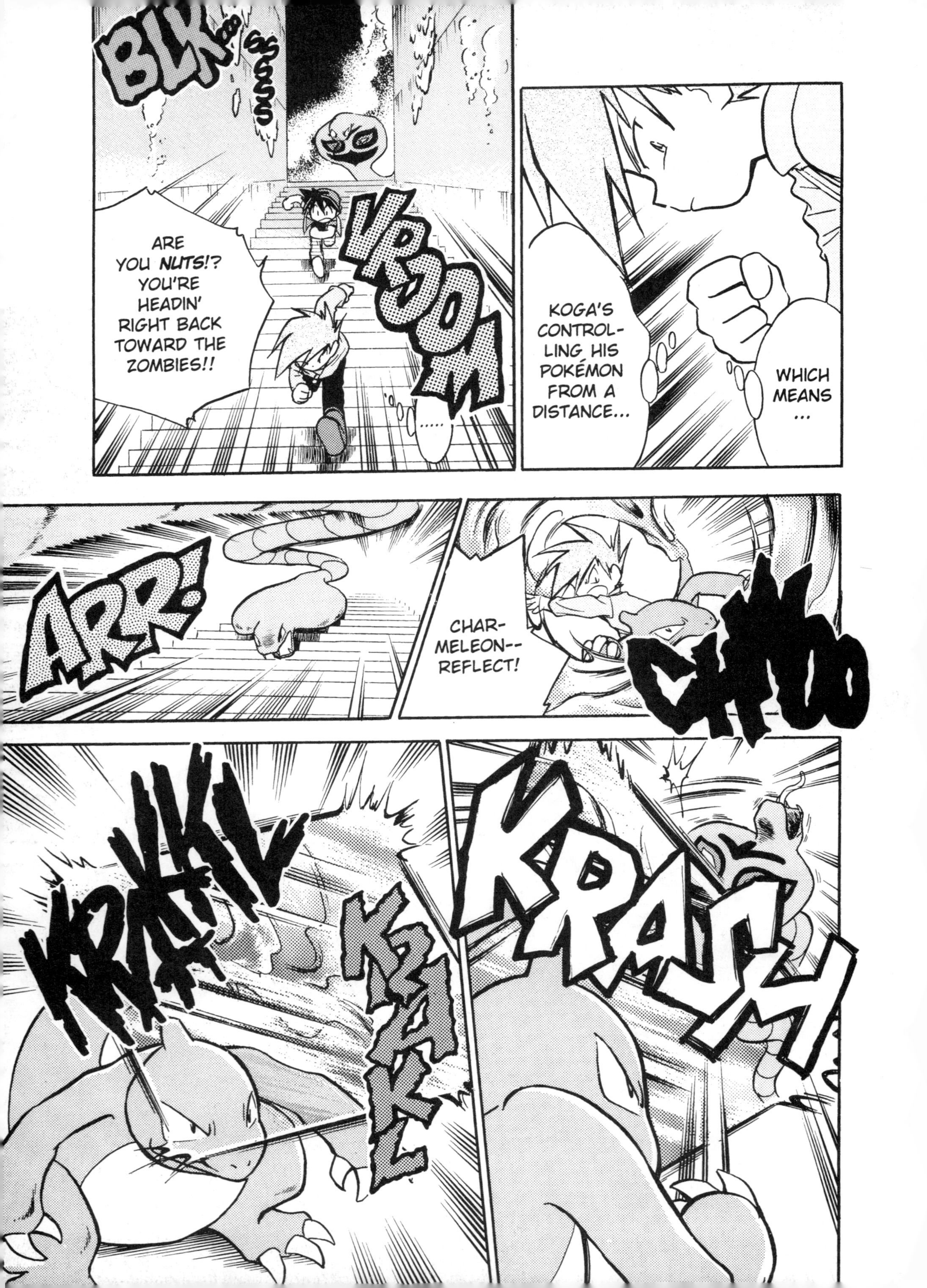
BLK
VROOM
ARE YOU **NUTS**!? YOU'RE HEADIN' RIGHT BACK TOWARD THE ZOMBIES!!
......
KOGA'S CONTROL-LING HIS POKÉMON FROM A DISTANCE...
WHICH MEANS ...
ARR!
CHAR-MELEON-- REFLECT!

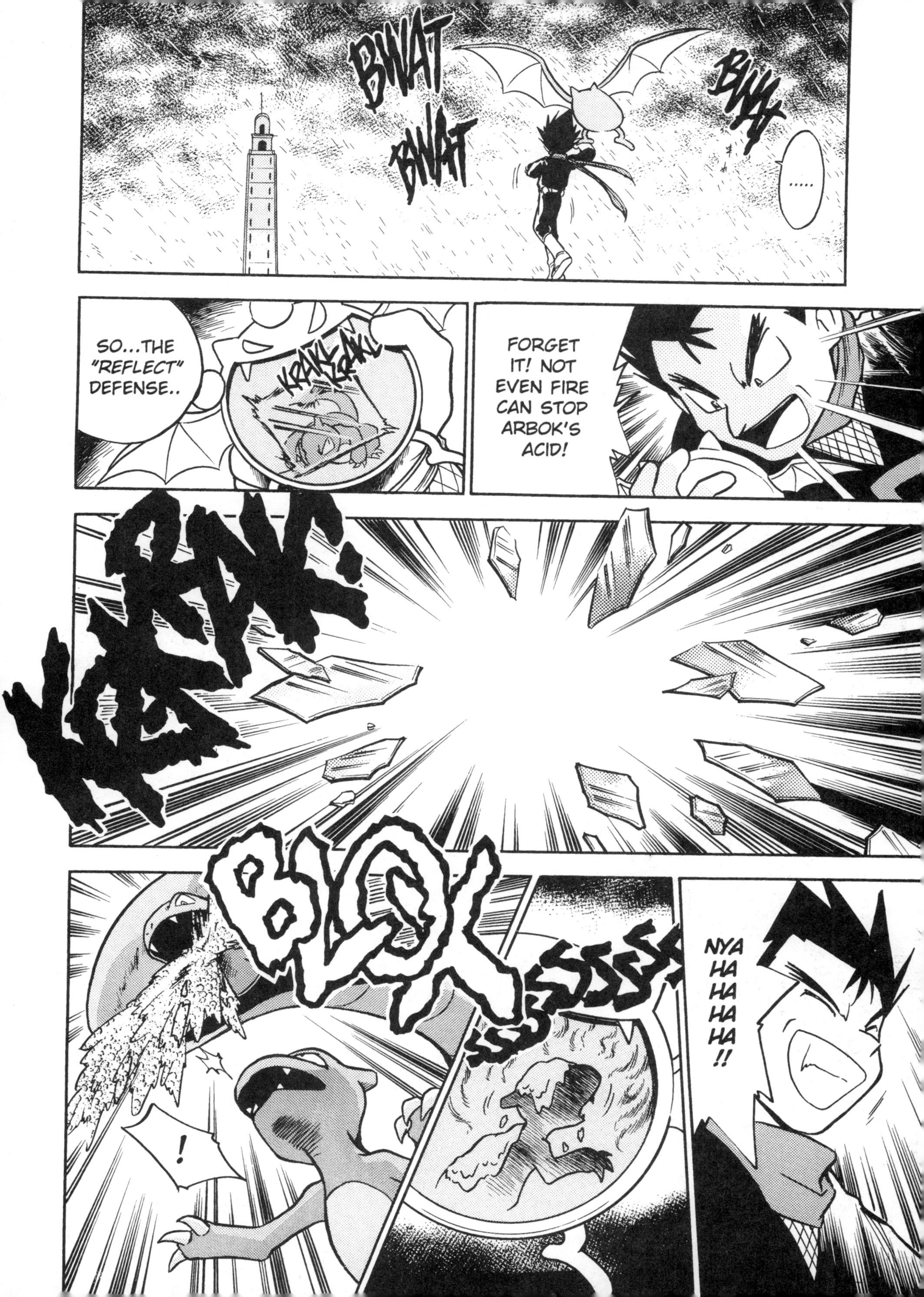
BWAT
BWAT
BWAT
BWAT
......
SO...THE "REFLECT" DEFENSE..
KRAK KRAK
FORGET IT! NOT EVEN FIRE CAN STOP ARBOK'S ACID!
NYA HA HA HA HA!!
!

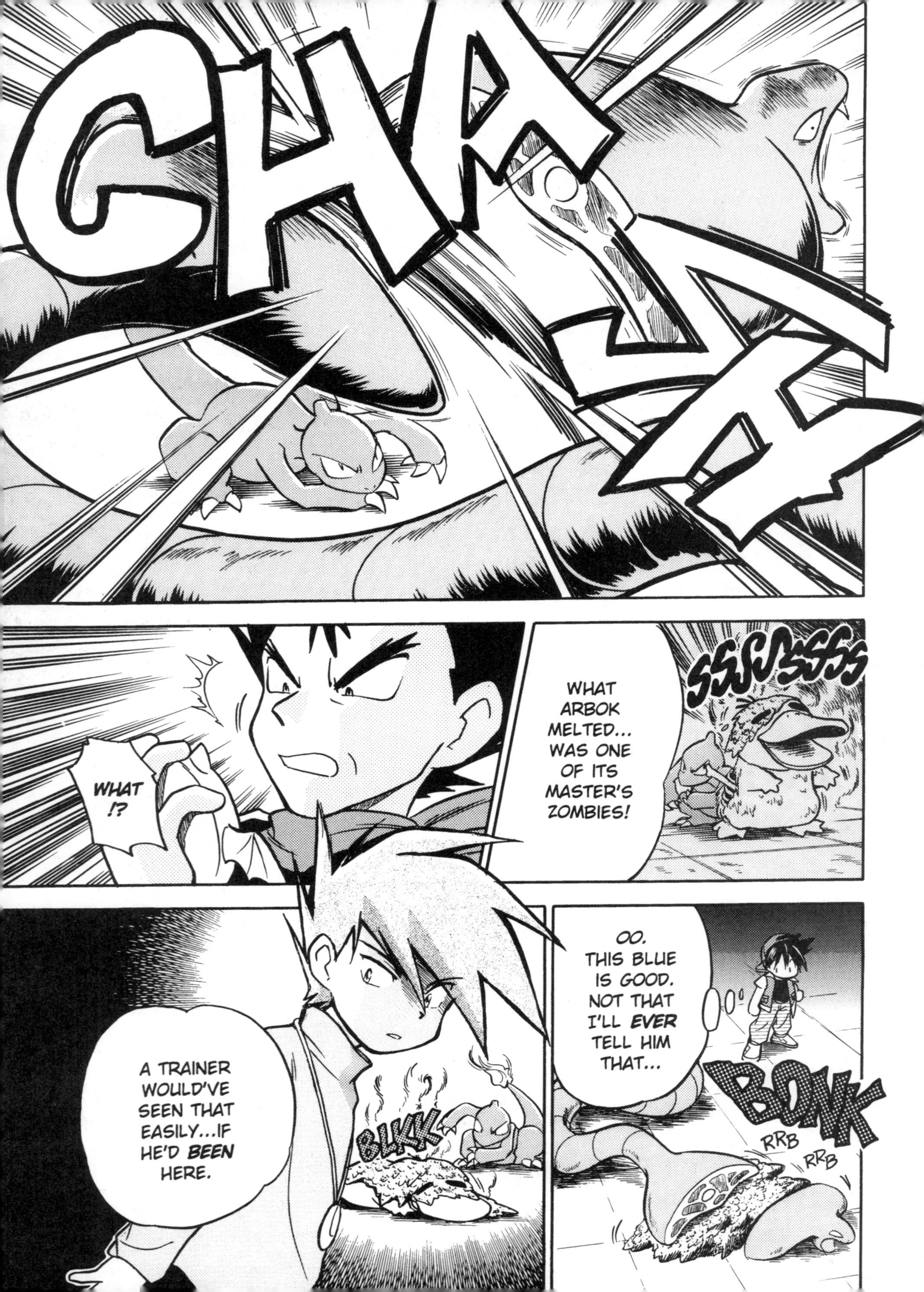
CHA
WHAT!?
WHAT ARBOK MELTED... WAS ONE OF ITS MASTER'S ZOMBIES!
SSSSSSSS
A TRAINER WOULD'VE SEEN THAT EASILY...IF HE'D BEEN HERE.
BLKK
OO. THIS BLUE IS GOOD. NOT THAT I'LL EVER TELL HIM THAT...
BONK
RRB
RRB

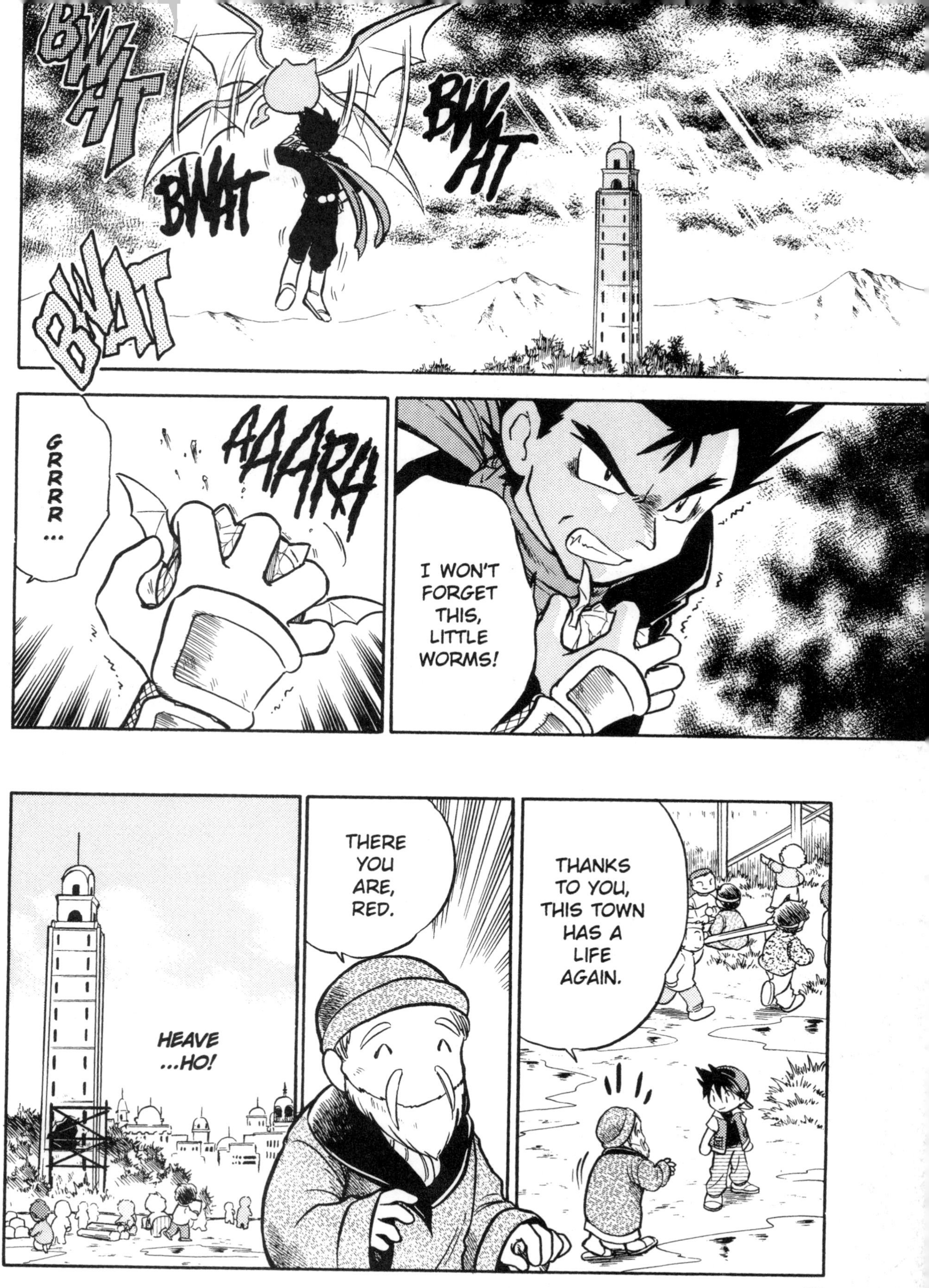
BWAT
BWAT
BWAT
BWAT
GRRRR...
AAARA
I WON'T FORGET THIS, LITTLE WORMS!
HEAVE ...HO!
THERE YOU ARE, RED.
THANKS TO YOU, THIS TOWN HAS A LIFE AGAIN.

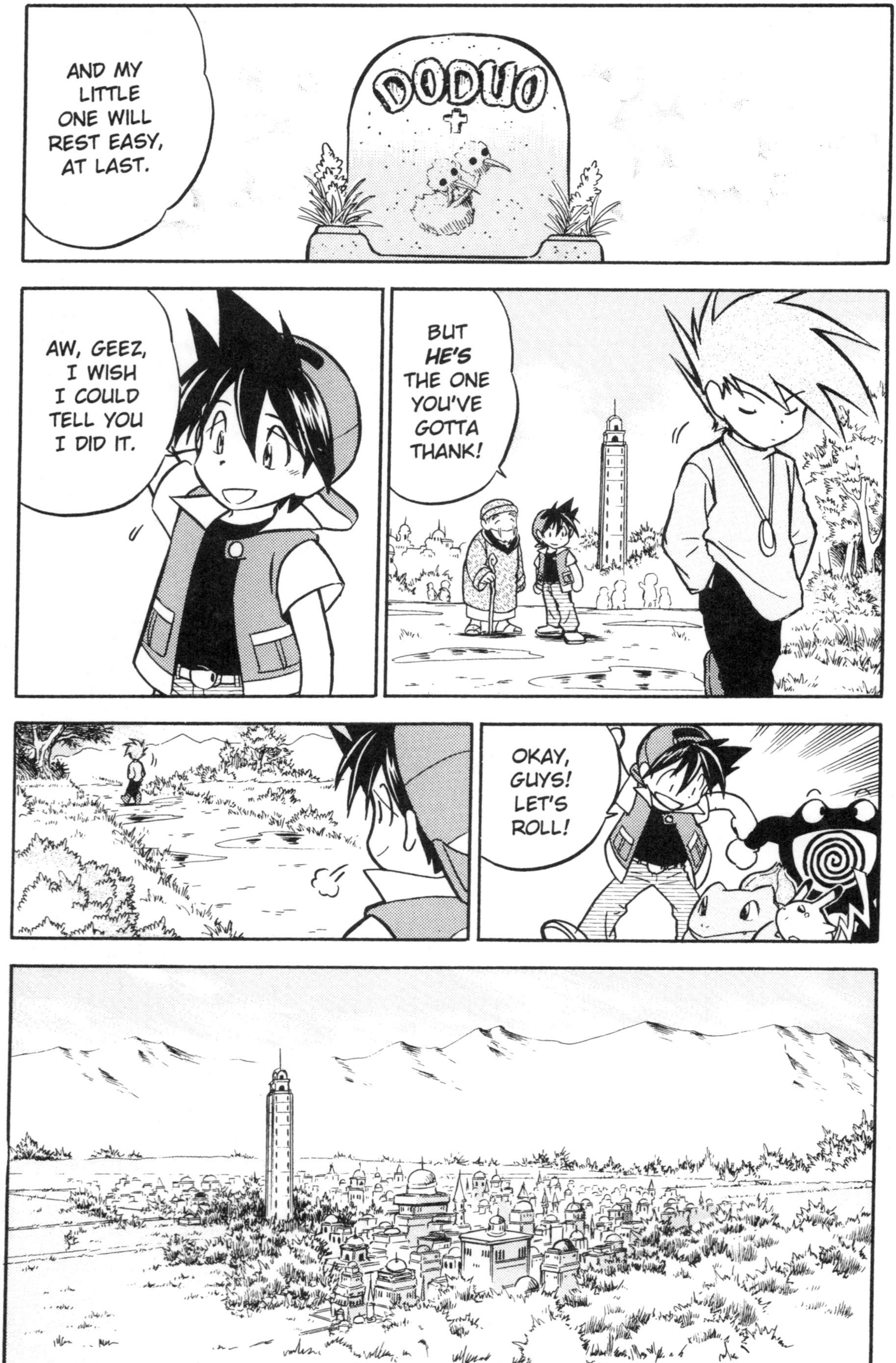
AND MY LITTLE ONE WILL REST EASY, AT LAST.
DODUO
AW, GEEZ, I WISH I COULD TELL YOU I DID IT.
BUT HE'S THE ONE YOU'VE GOTTA THANK!
OKAY, GUYS! LET'S ROLL!

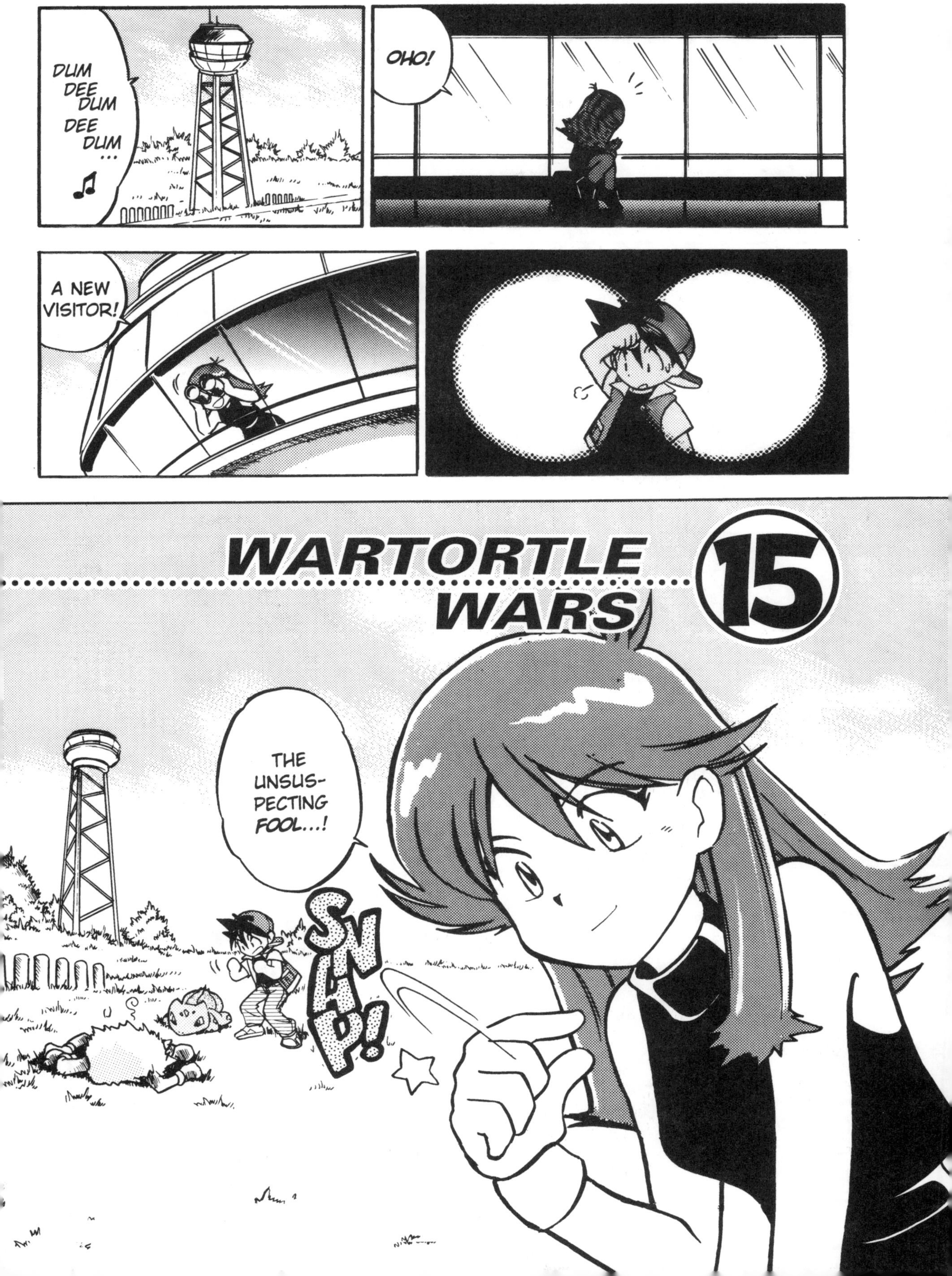
DUM DEE DUM DEE DUM ...
OHO!
A NEW VISITOR!
WARTORTLE WARS
15
THE UNSUS-PECTING FOOL...!
SNAP!

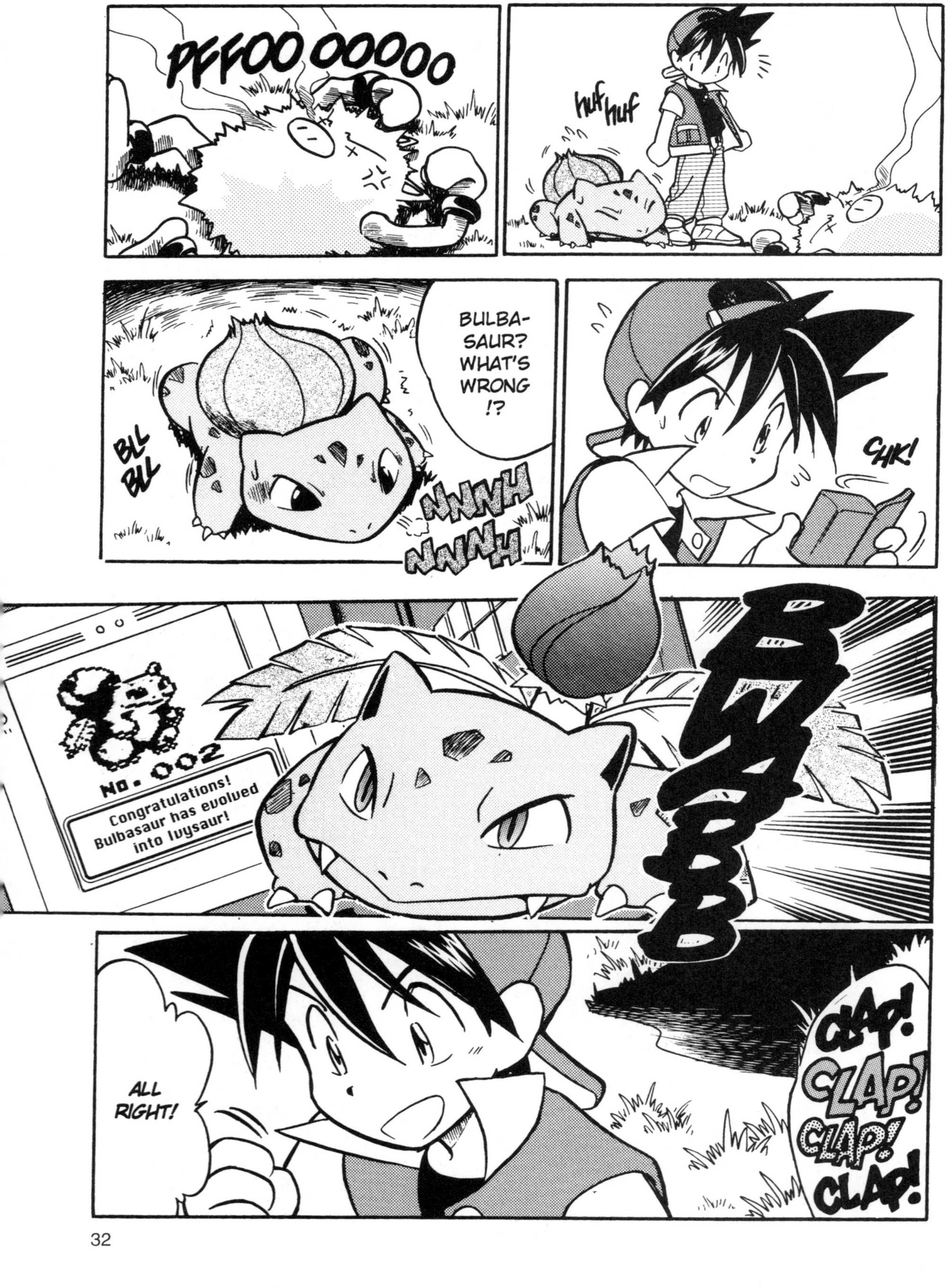
PFFOO OOOOO
huf huf
BULBA-SAUR? WHAT'S WRONG !?
BLL BLL
NNNH NNNH
CHK!
NO. 002
Congratulations! Bulbasaur has evolved into Ivysaur!
BWOBBB
ALL RIGHT!
CLAP! CLAP! CLAP! CLAP!

WHO
--?

OOO! THAT WAS AWE- SOME!

CONGRAT- ULATIONS TO YOU BOTH!

HUH? UH. YEAH. THANKS.

YOU MUST BE **SUCH A GOOD** POKEMON TRAINER! ♡

I GOT **SO** EXCITED WATCHING YOU BATTLE! ♡

W-- WELL, I **TRY**.

TCH. TOO BAD.

IF ONLY YOU HAD SOME POKÉMON ITEMS...

ITEMS ...?

YOU KNOW! TO MAKE YOUR POKÉMON EVEN STRONGER! ♡

TADAAAAAAAA

THIS **POWER PLUS** WILL ENHANCE ATTACK- POWER. AND THIS ONE... ♡

BLAH BLAH

I-I-I'M SURE THEY'RE GR-- GREAT, B-BUT....

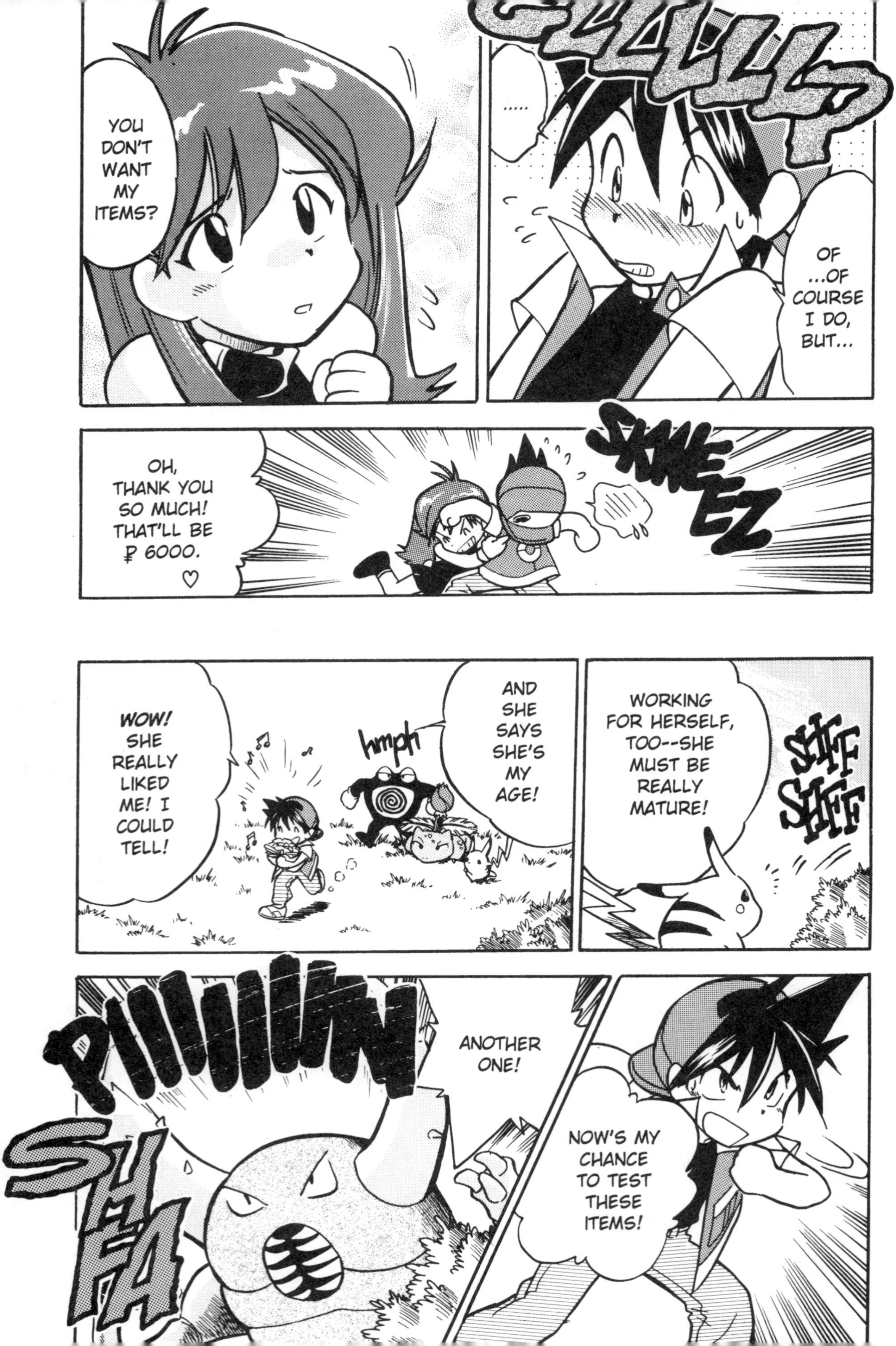
YOU DON'T WANT MY ITEMS?
GLLLLP
.....
OF ...OF COURSE I DO, BUT...
OH, THANK YOU SO MUCH! THAT'LL BE ₽ 6000. ♡
SKWEEZ
WOW! SHE REALLY LIKED ME! I COULD TELL!
hmph
AND SHE SAYS SHE'S MY AGE!
WORKING FOR HERSELF, TOO--SHE MUST BE REALLY MATURE!
SNIFF SNIFF
PWWWWN
SHFA
ANOTHER ONE!
NOW'S MY CHANCE TO TEST THESE ITEMS!

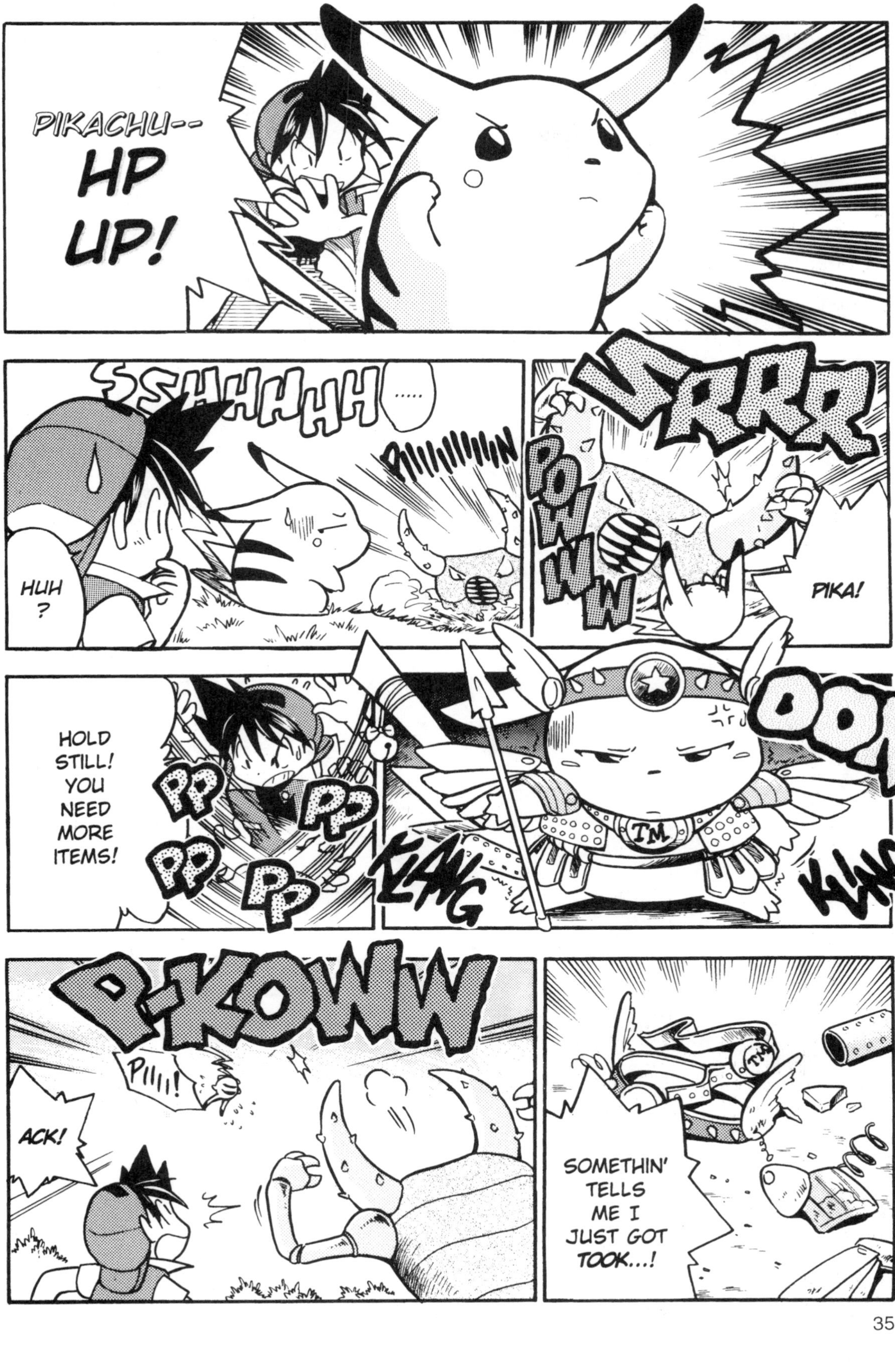
PIKACHU--
HP UP!
SSHHHHHH
......
HUH ?
PIIIIIIIIN
SRRR
POWWWNN
PIKA!
HOLD STILL! YOU NEED MORE ITEMS!
PP
PP
PP
PP
KLANG
OOM
KLANG
TM
P-KOWW
PIIII!
ACK!
SOMETHIN' TELLS ME I JUST GOT TOOK...!

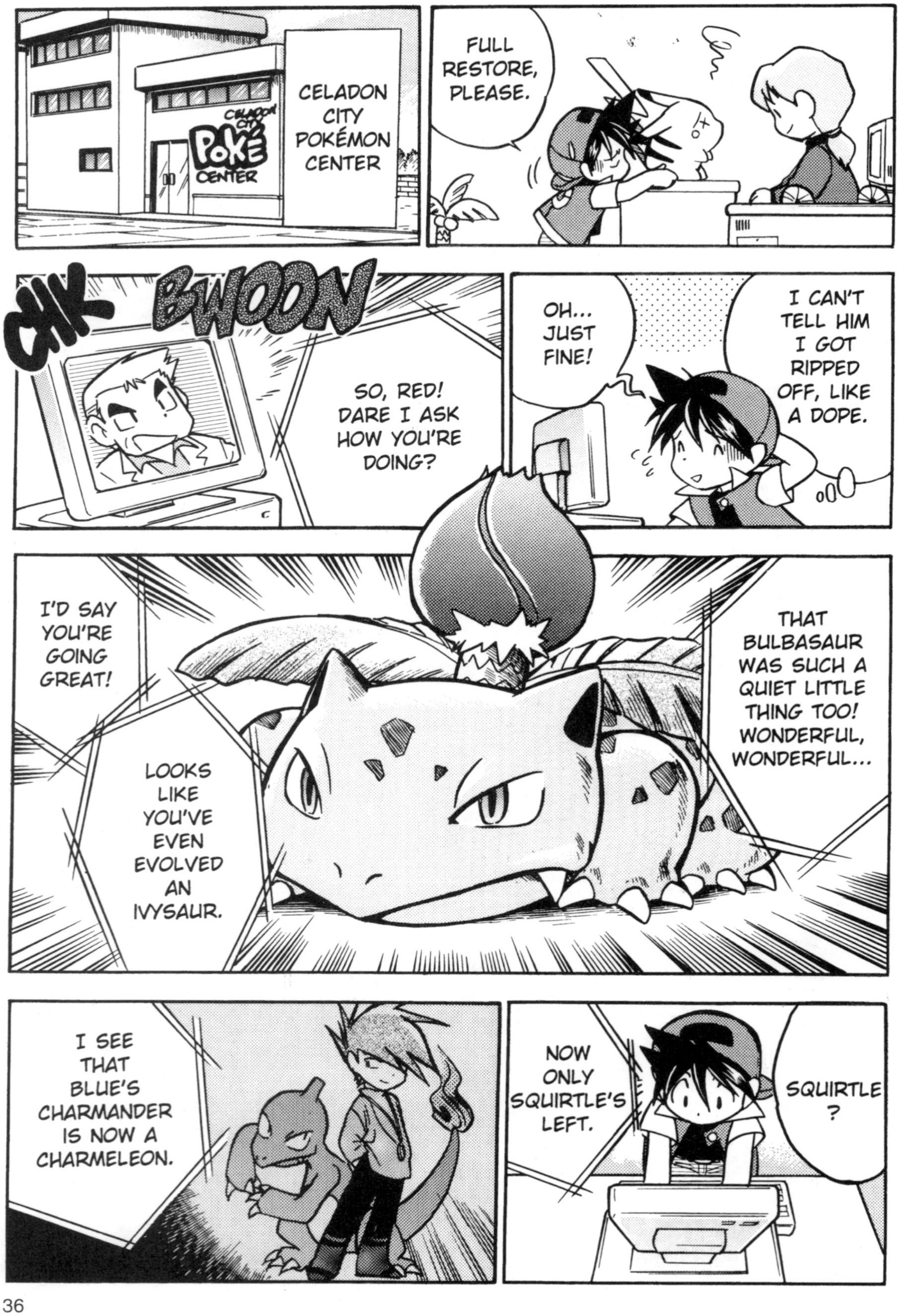
CELADON CITY POKÉMON CENTER
CELADON CITY POKÉ CENTER
FULL RESTORE, PLEASE.
CHK
BWOON
SO, RED! DARE I ASK HOW YOU'RE DOING?
OH... JUST FINE!
I CAN'T TELL HIM I GOT RIPPED OFF, LIKE A DOPE.
I'D SAY YOU'RE GOING GREAT!
LOOKS LIKE YOU'VE EVEN EVOLVED AN IVYSAUR.
THAT BULBASAUR WAS SUCH A QUIET LITTLE THING TOO! WONDERFUL, WONDERFUL...
I SEE THAT BLUE'S CHARMANDER IS NOW A CHARMELEON.
NOW ONLY SQUIRTLE'S LEFT.
SQUIRTLE?

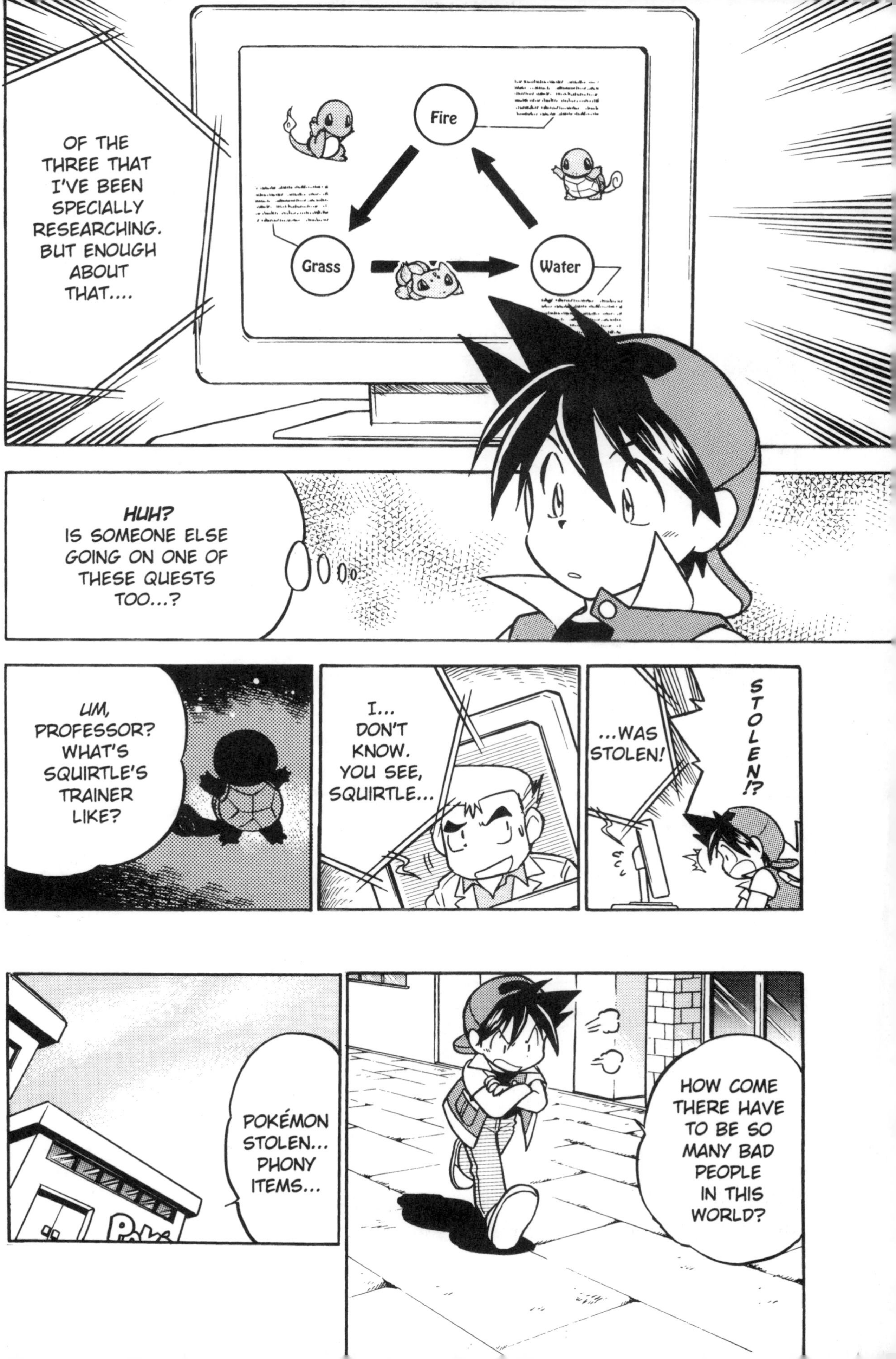

Fire
Grass
Water
OF THE THREE THAT I'VE BEEN SPECIALLY RESEARCHING. BUT ENOUGH ABOUT THAT....
HUH? IS SOMEONE ELSE GOING ON ONE OF THESE QUESTS TOO...?
UM, PROFESSOR? WHAT'S SQUIRTLE'S TRAINER LIKE?
I... DON'T KNOW. YOU SEE, SQUIRTLE...
...WAS STOLEN!
STOLEN!?
HOW COME THERE HAVE TO BE SO MANY BAD PEOPLE IN THIS WORLD?
POKÉMON STOLEN... PHONY ITEMS...

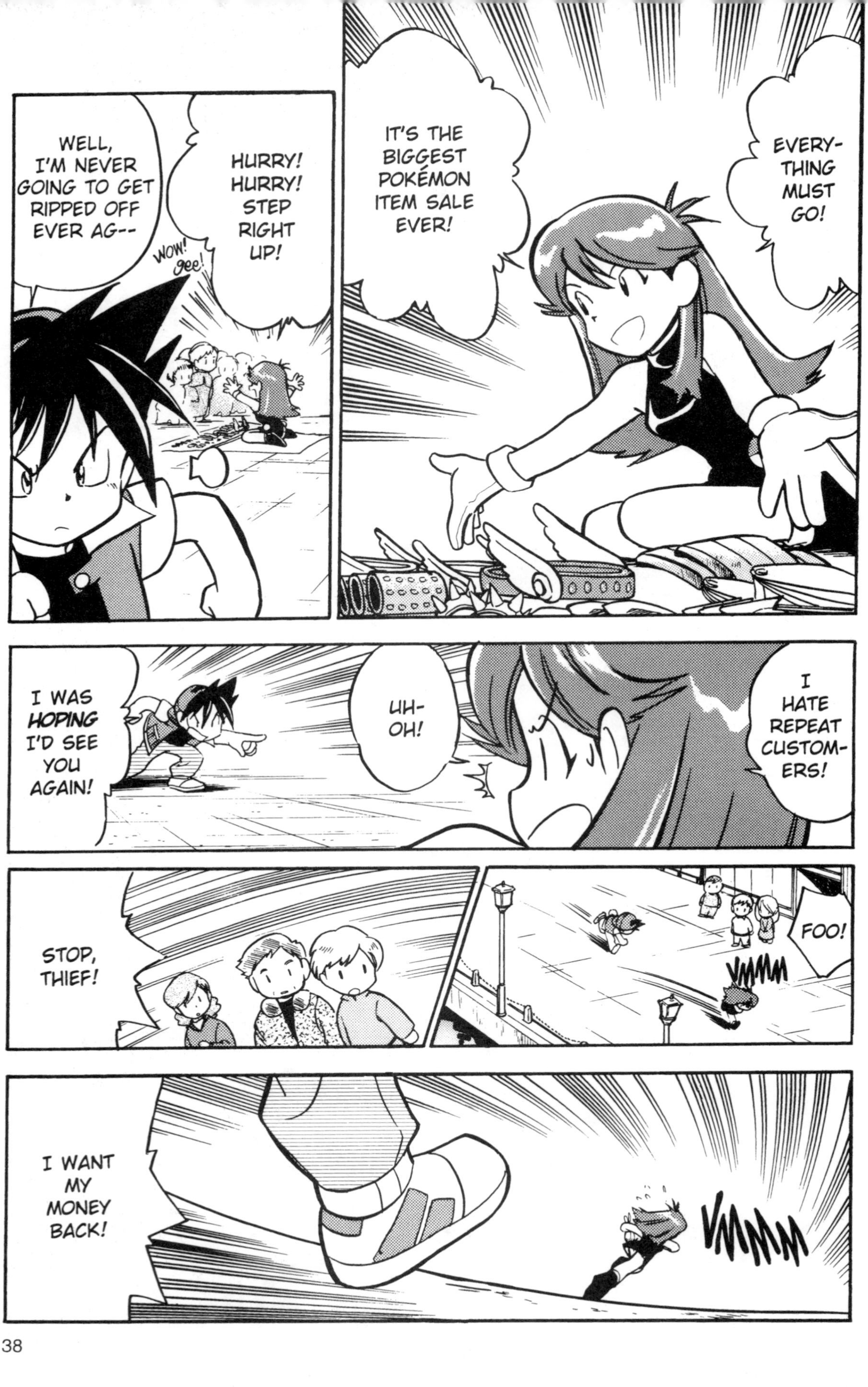
EVERY-THING MUST GO!
IT'S THE BIGGEST POKÉMON ITEM SALE EVER!
HURRY! HURRY! STEP RIGHT UP!
WOW! gee!
WELL, I'M NEVER GOING TO GET RIPPED OFF EVER AG--
I HATE REPEAT CUSTOM-ERS!
UH-OH!
I WAS HOPING I'D SEE YOU AGAIN!
FOO!
VMMM
STOP, THIEF!
VMMM
I WANT MY MONEY BACK!

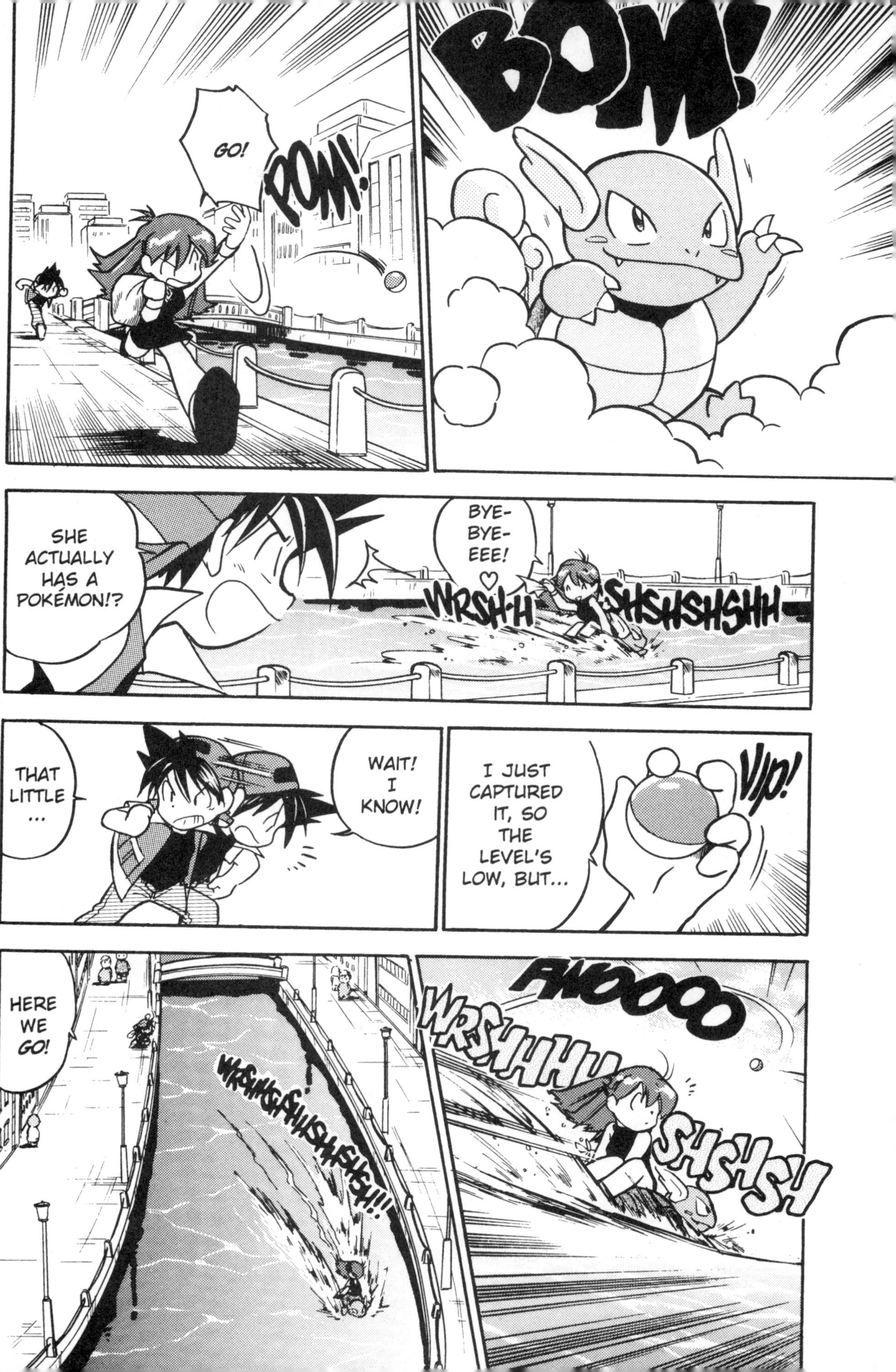
GO!
POM!
BOM!
SHE ACTUALLY HAS A POKÉMON!?
BYE-BYE-EEE! ♡
WRSH-H
SHSHSHSHH
THAT LITTLE ...
WAIT! I KNOW!
I JUST CAPTURED IT, SO THE LEVEL'S LOW, BUT...
VIP!
HERE WE GO!
RWOOOO
WRSHHHH
SHSHSH
WRSHHSHSHSHSHSHSH!!

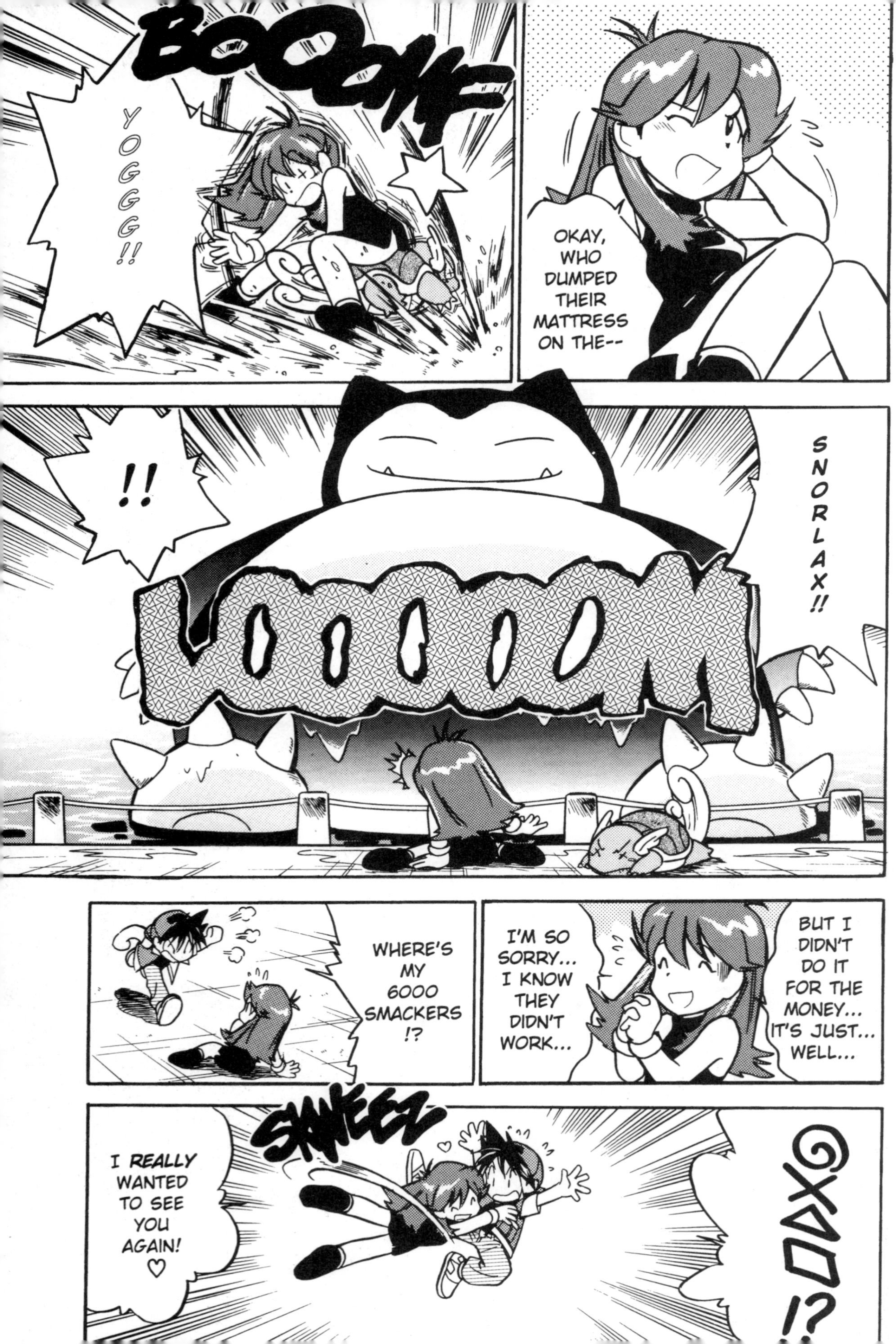
BOOOMF
YOGGG!!
OKAY, WHO DUMPED THEIR MATTRESS ON THE--
!!
SNORLAX!!
VOOOOOM
WHERE'S MY 6000 SMACKERS !?
I'M SO SORRY... I KNOW THEY DIDN'T WORK...
BUT I DIDN'T DO IT FOR THE MONEY... IT'S JUST... WELL...
SKWEEZ
I **REALLY** WANTED TO SEE YOU AGAIN! ♡
GXAAA!?

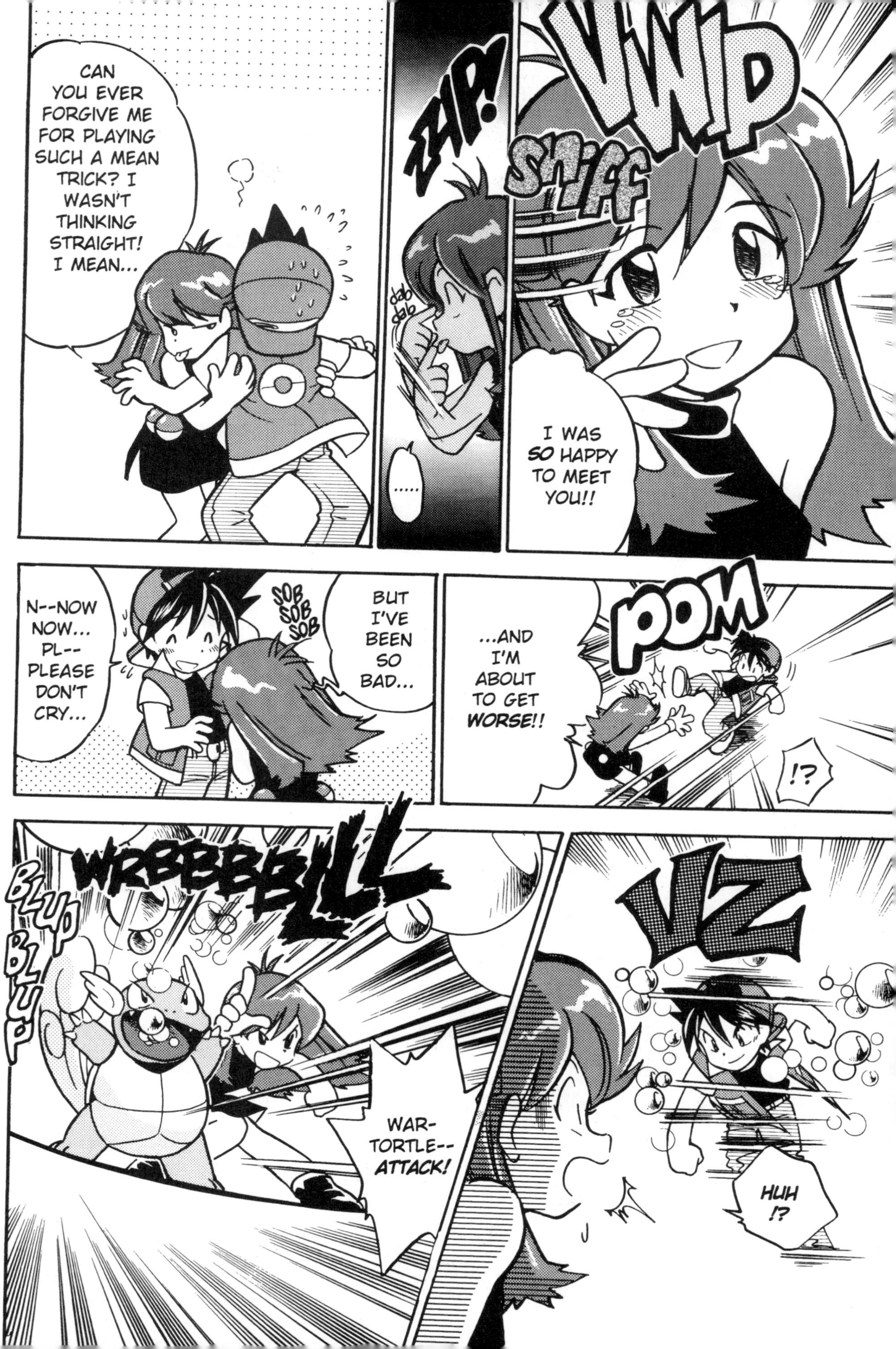

CAN YOU EVER FORGIVE ME FOR PLAYING SUCH A MEAN TRICK? I WASN'T THINKING STRAIGHT! I MEAN...
ZIP!
dab dab
......
VWIP
SNIFF
I WAS SO HAPPY TO MEET YOU!!
N--NOW NOW... PL--PLEASE DON'T CRY...
SOB SOB SOB
BUT I'VE BEEN SO BAD...
...AND I'M ABOUT TO GET WORSE!!
POM
!?
BLUP BLUP BLUP
WRBBBBLLL
WAR-TORTLE--ATTACK!
VZ
HUH!?

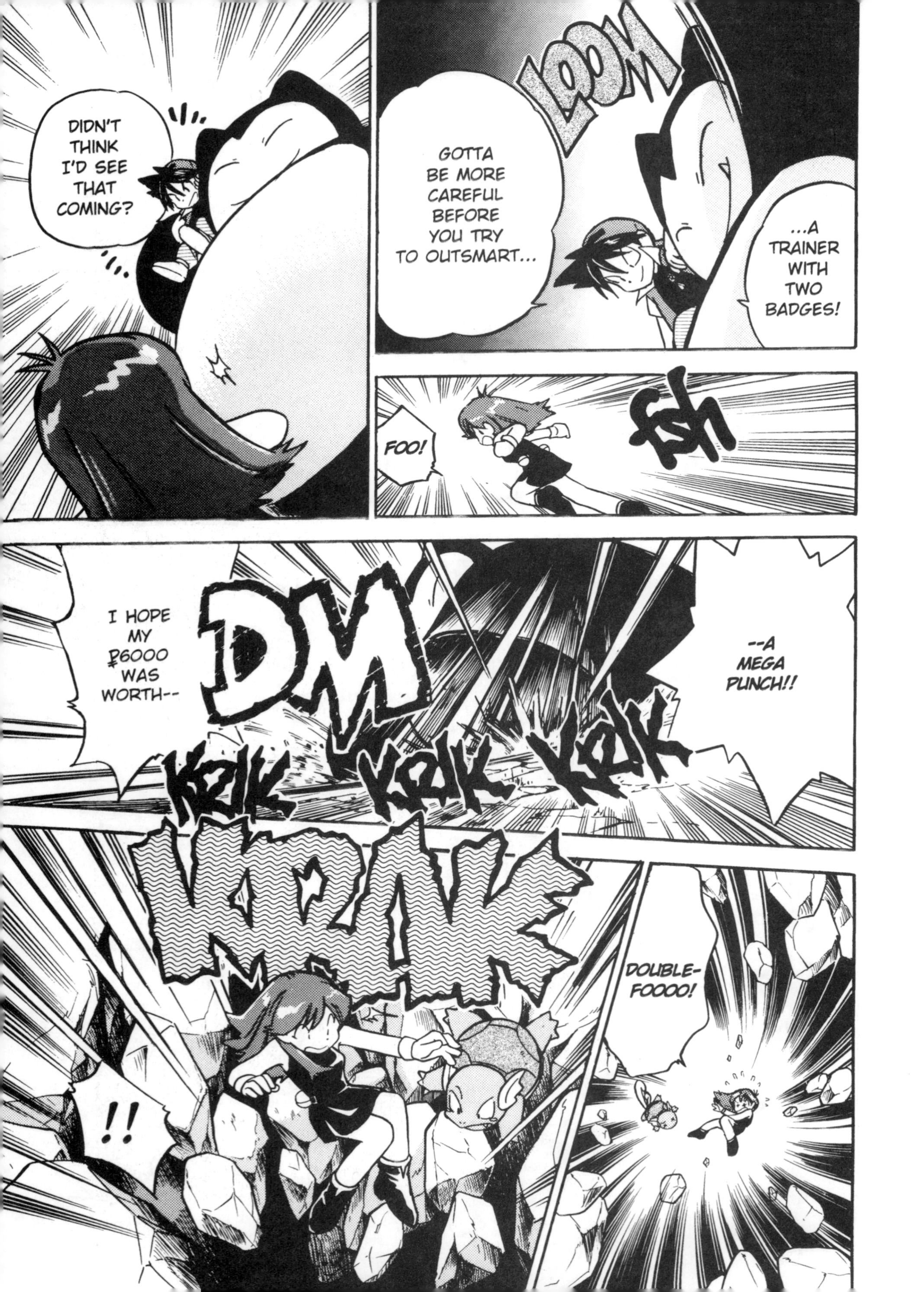
DIDN'T THINK I'D SEE THAT COMING?
GOTTA BE MORE CAREFUL BEFORE YOU TRY TO OUTSMART...
...A TRAINER WITH TWO BADGES!
LOOM
FOO!
fsh
I HOPE MY ₽6000 WAS WORTH--
DM
--A MEGA PUNCH!!
KRIK KRIK KRIK
KRAK
DOUBLE-FOOOO!
!!

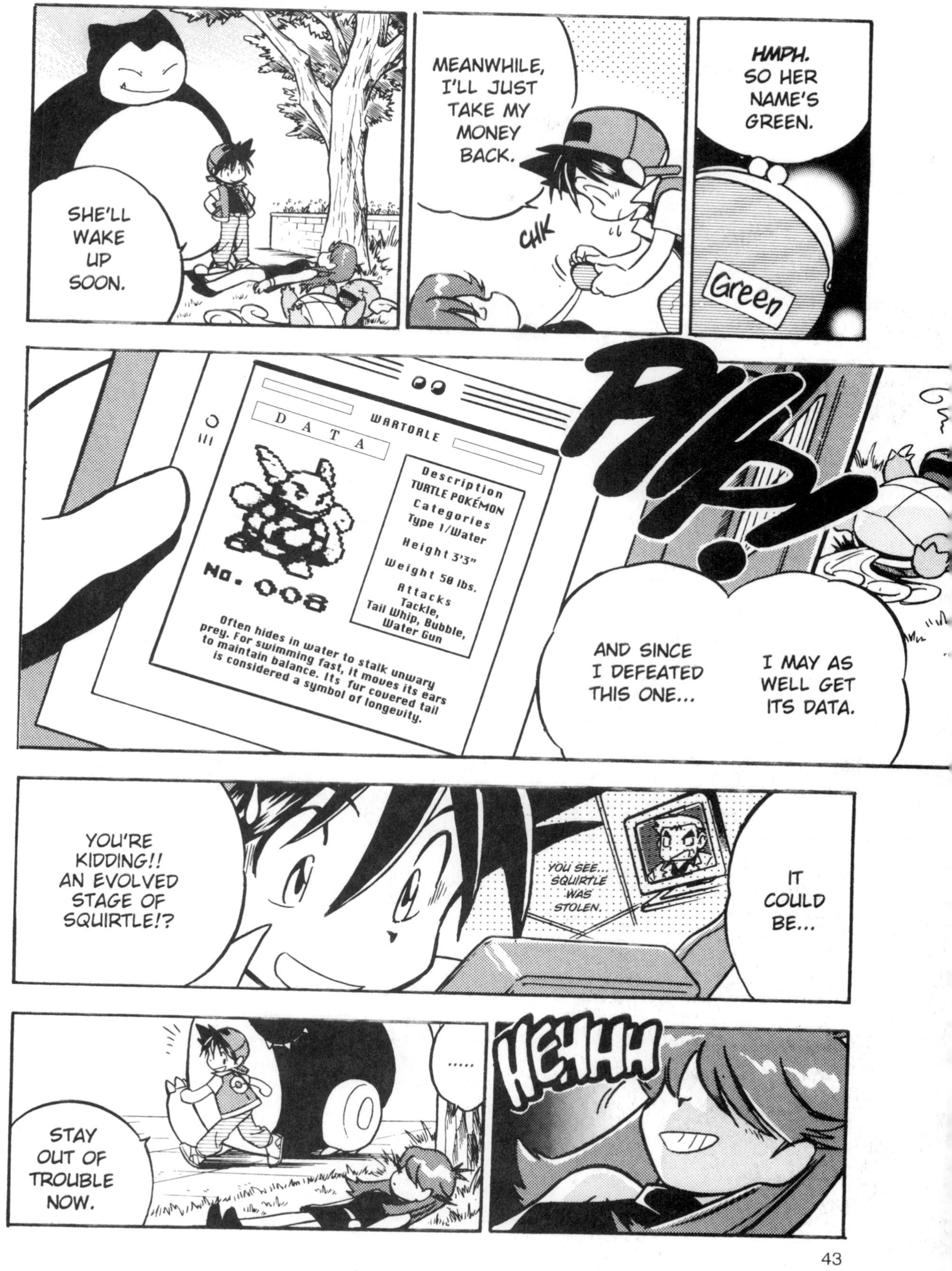
SHE'LL WAKE UP SOON.
MEANWHILE, I'LL JUST TAKE MY MONEY BACK.
CHK
HMPH. SO HER NAME'S GREEN.
Green
DATA
WARTORLE
Description
TURTLE POKÉMON
Categories
Type 1/Water
Height 3'3"
Weight 50 lbs.
Attacks
Tackle, Tail Whip, Bubble, Water Gun
No. 008
Often hides in water to stalk unwary prey. For swimming fast, it moves its ears to maintain balance. Its fur covered tail is considered a symbol of longevity.
PIBY!
AND SINCE I DEFEATED THIS ONE...
I MAY AS WELL GET ITS DATA.
YOU'RE KIDDING!! AN EVOLVED STAGE OF SQUIRTLE!?
YOU SEE... SQUIRTLE WAS STOLEN.
IT COULD BE...
STAY OUT OF TROUBLE NOW.
.....
HEHHH

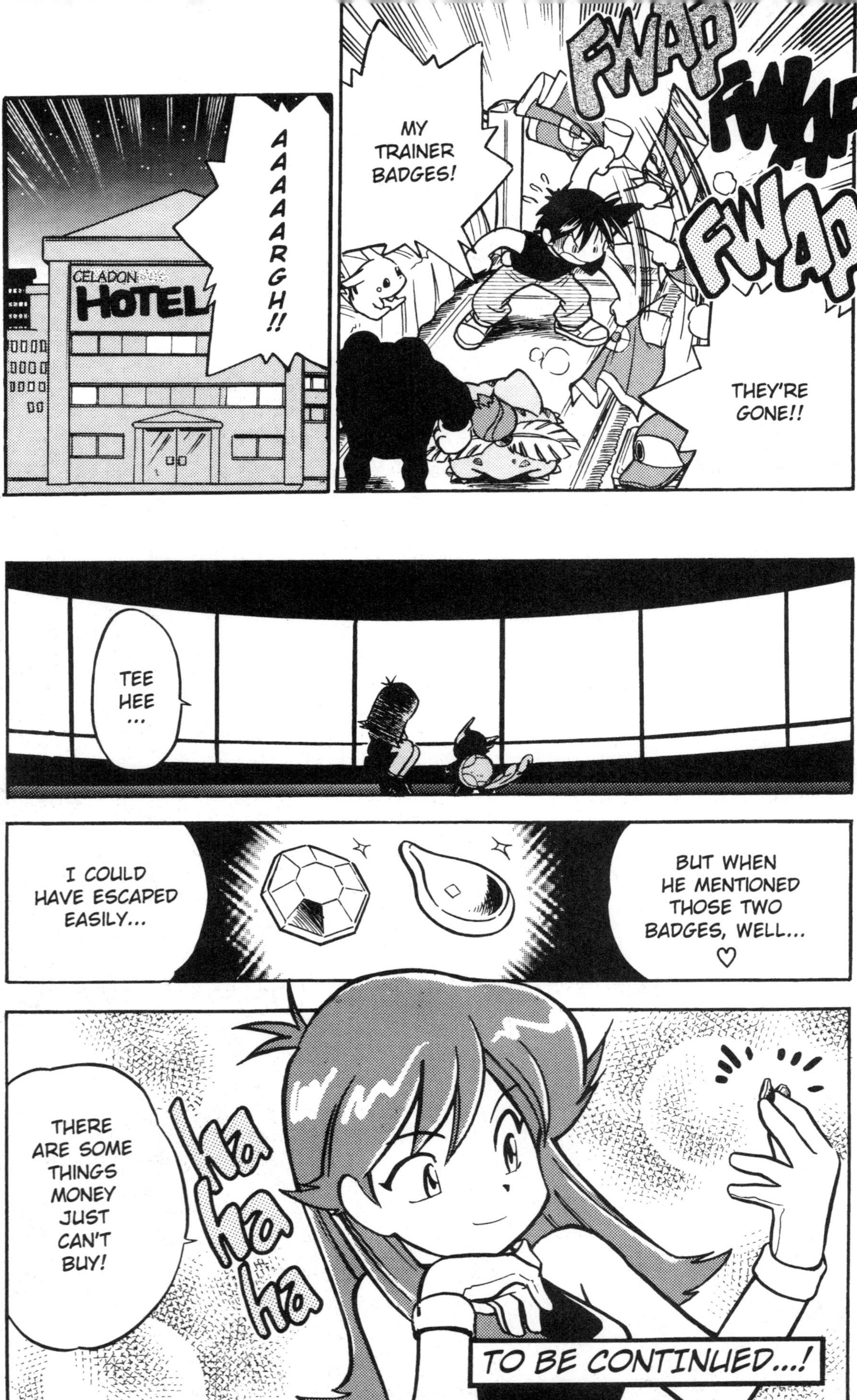
AAAAAARGH!!
CELADON HOTEL
MY TRAINER BADGES!
FWAP FWAP FWAP
THEY'RE GONE!!
TEE HEE ...
I COULD HAVE ESCAPED EASILY...
BUT WHEN HE MENTIONED THOSE TWO BADGES, WELL... ♡
THERE ARE SOME THINGS MONEY JUST CAN'T BUY!
ha ha ha ha
TO BE CONTINUED...!

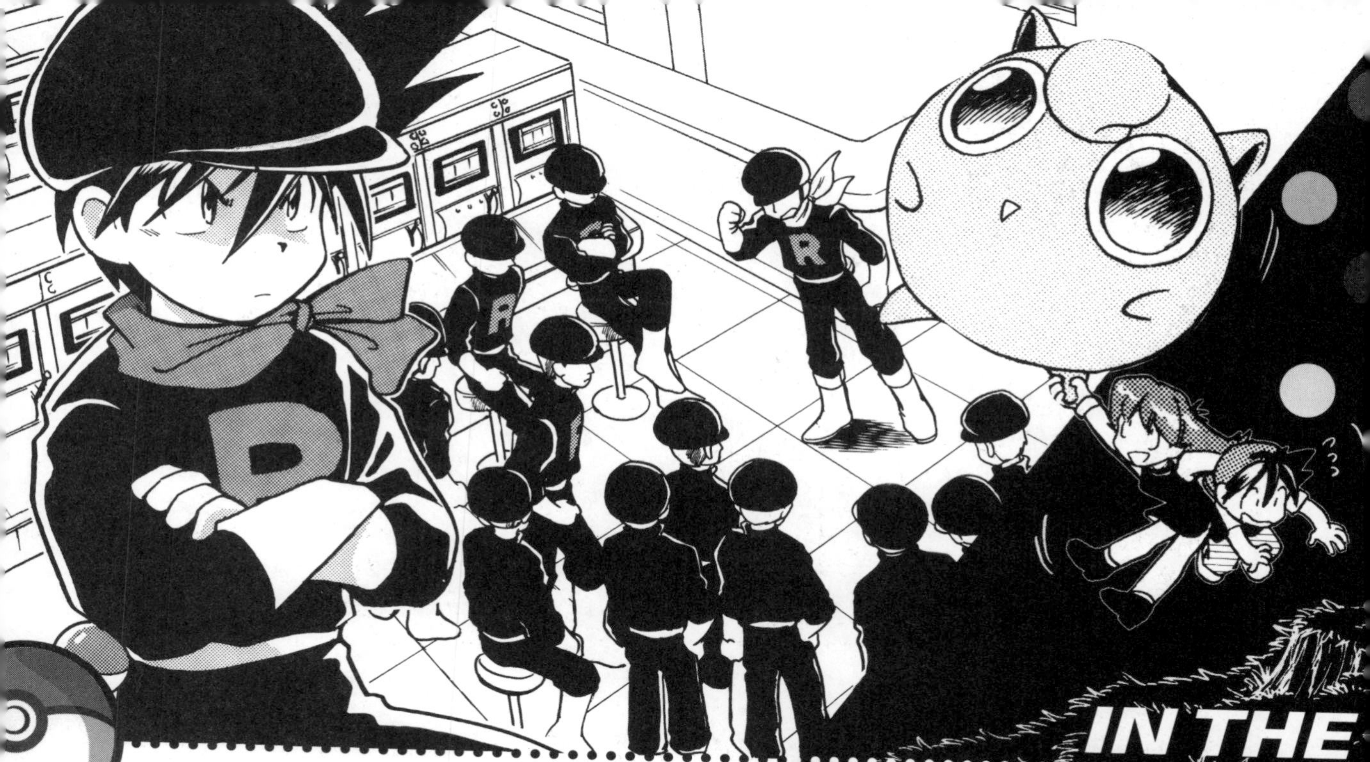

IN THE NEXT ISSUE:

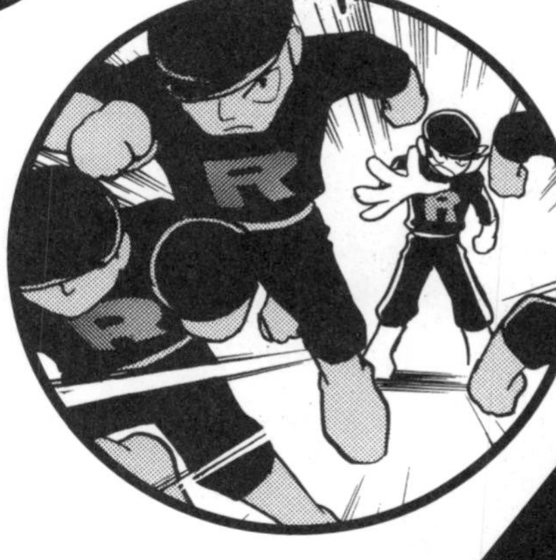

- Team Rocket is after Green! What's she done now!?
- See Red in disguise!
- What is Team Rocket's villainous plan?

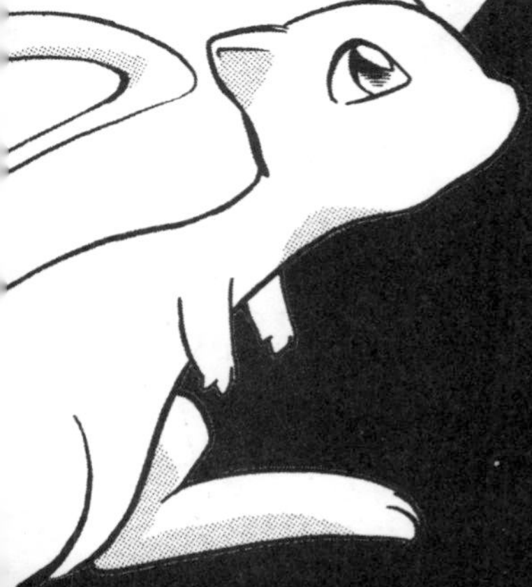

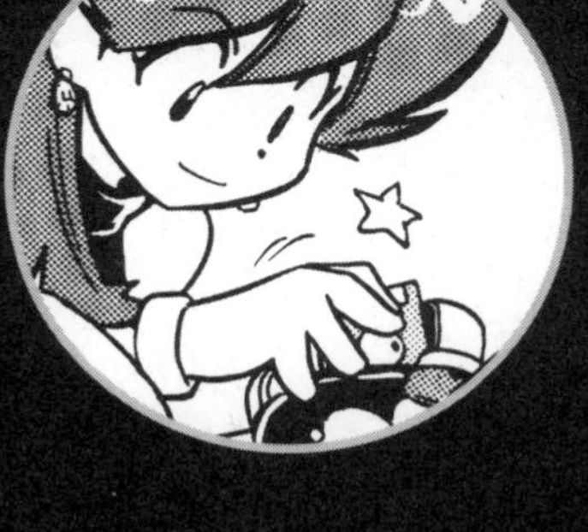

- Green's got some great gadgets!
- An appearance by Mew!

Get the next exciting issue:
Team Rocket Returns on sale soon!

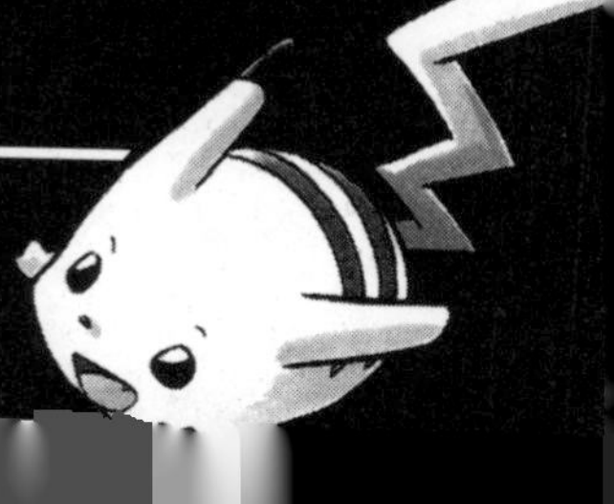

into a panda, and the weird Chinese curse that did it to 'em!

Rumiko Takahashi's Ranma 1/2™

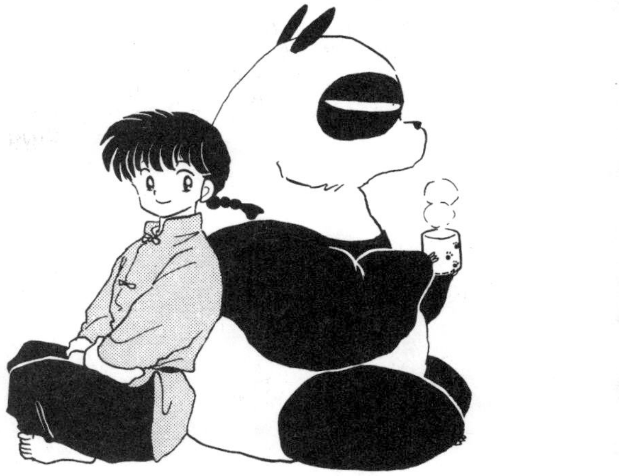

Ranma 1/2 ©1999 Rumiko Takahashi/Shogakukan, Inc.

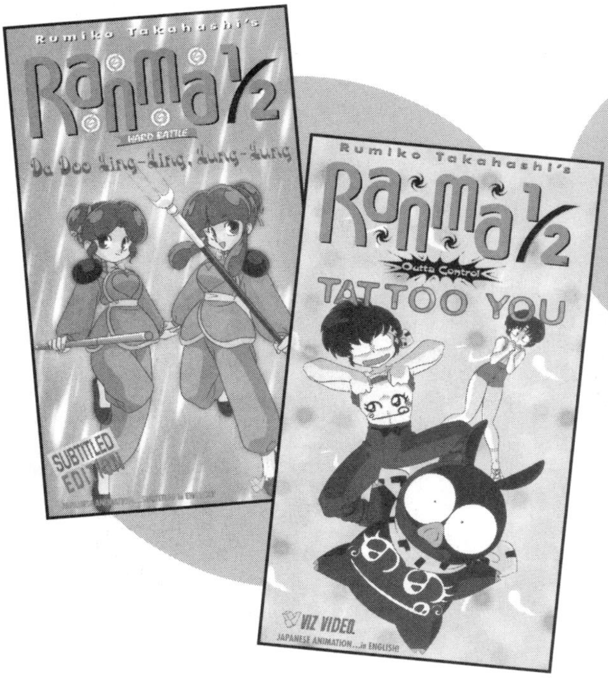
Rumiko Takahashi's
Ranma 1/2
HARD BATTLE
Da Doo Ling-Ling, Lung-Lung
SUBTITLED EDITION
Rumiko Takahashi's
Ranma 1/2
Outta Control
TATTOO YOU
VIZ VIDEO
JAPANESE ANIMATION...in ENGLISH!

Videos!

Four seasons of the anime TV series, plus movies and original animated videos. Available in English or in Japanese with English subtitles.

TITLE	ENGLISH	SUBTITLED
Original TV Series (Vols. 1-9)	$29.95 ea.	n/a
Collector's Edition TV Series (Vols. 1-6)	n/a	$34.95 ea.
Anything-Goes Martial Arts (Vols. 1-11)	$24.95 ea.	$29.95 ea.
Hard Battle (Vols. 1-12)	$24.95 ea.	$29.95 ea.
Outta Control (Vols. 1-12)	$24.95 ea.	Coming Soon
OAVs Vols. 1-6 (Vols. 1-3 are English-only)	$29.95 ea.	$29.95 ea.
Collector's Editions OAVs (Vols. 1-2)	n/a	$34.95 ea.
Video Jukebox	n/a	$14.95 ea.
Movie: Big Trouble in Nekonron, China	$34.95 ea.	$34.95 ea.
2nd Movie: Nihao My Concubine	$34.95 ea.	$34.95 ea.
Digital Dojo Box Set (9 Vols.)	$199.95 ea.	n/a
Anything-Goes Box Set (11 Vols.)	$199.95 ea.	n/a
OAV Box Set (6 Vols.)	$124.95 ea.	n/a
Hard Battle Box Set (12 Vols.)	$199.95 ea.	n/a

Plus!

Graphic Novels: 13 volumes & counting!
T-Shirts: 7 styles available in different sizes!
Music: 6 soundtracks from the anime TV series and movies.
Monthly Comics: Available by subscription or individual issues!
Merchandise: Baseball caps, Cappuccino mugs, watches, postcards & more!

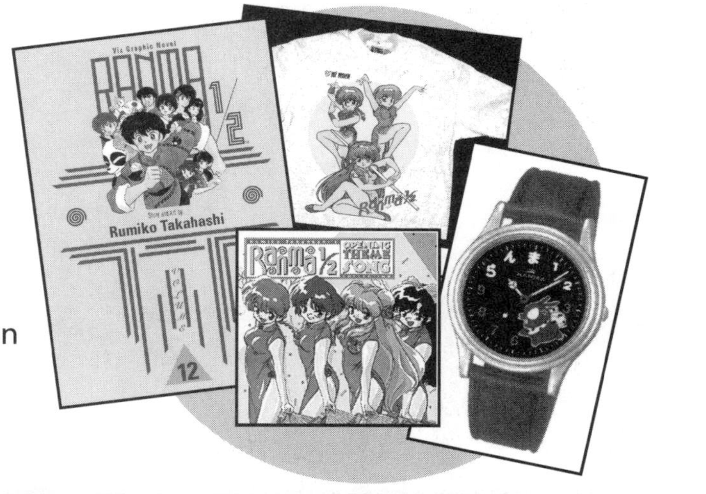
Viz Graphic Novel
RANMA 1/2
Rumiko Takahashi
12
Ranma 1/2
OPENING THEME SONG

AVAILABLE AT YOUR LOCAL COMICS STORE!
Or order online at WWW.J-POP.COM
PHONE: (800) 394-3042 • FAX: (415) 546-7086
CALL US FOR THE LATEST RANMA VIDEOS!

VIZ COMICS™

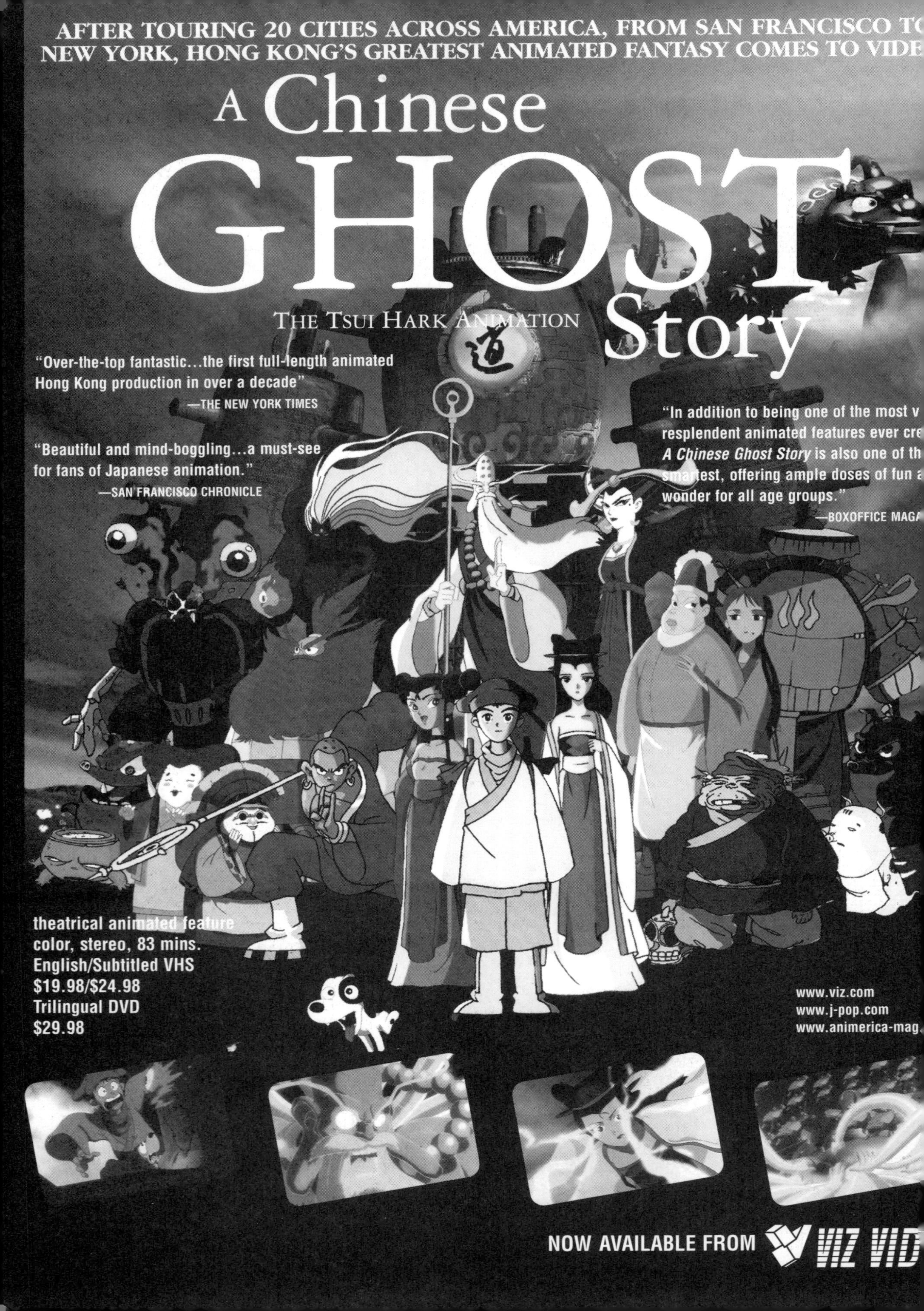
AFTER TOURING 20 CITIES ACROSS AMERICA, FROM SAN FRANCISCO TO
NEW YORK, HONG KONG'S GREATEST ANIMATED FANTASY COMES TO VIDE
A Chinese
GHOST
Story
THE TSUI HARK ANIMATION
道
"Over-the-top fantastic...the first full-length animated Hong Kong production in over a decade"
—THE NEW YORK TIMES
"Beautiful and mind-boggling...a must-see for fans of Japanese animation."
—SAN FRANCISCO CHRONICLE
"In addition to being one of the most v
resplendent animated features ever cre
A Chinese Ghost Story is also one of th
smartest, offering ample doses of fun a
wonder for all age groups."
—BOXOFFICE MAGA
theatrical animated feature
color, stereo, 83 mins.
English/Subtitled VHS
$19.98/$24.98
Trilingual DVD
$29.98
www.viz.com
www.j-pop.com
www.animerica-mag.
NOW AVAILABLE FROM VIZ VID